Charles King

Cadet Days

a Story of West Point

Charles King

Cadet Days
a Story of West Point

ISBN/EAN: 9783743305243

Manufactured in Europe, USA, Canada, Australia, Japa

Cover: Foto ©Andreas Hilbeck / pixelio.de

Manufactured and distributed by brebook publishing software
(www.brebook.com)

Charles King

Cadet Days

"HE IS LIFTED ON THEIR SHOULDERS AND BORNE DOWN THE ROAD"

CADET DAYS

A Story of West Point

BY

CAPTAIN CHARLES KING, U.S.A.

AUTHOR OF

"A WAR-TIME WOOING" "BETWEEN THE LINES"
"CAMPAIGNING WITH CROOK" ETC.

ILLUSTRATED

NEW YORK
HARPER & BROTHERS PUBLISHERS

TO

A MOTHER

WHO GAVE HER ONLY SON TO OUR ARMY, WHO LIVED FOR HIM
THROUGH TRIAL TO FINAL TRIUMPH, AND WHO EVEN IN
HER SADDEST DAYS, BROUGHT HOPE TO OTHER
HEARTS AND SUNSHINE TO OTHER HOMES
THIS STORY OF CADET LIFE

Is Inscribed

ILLUSTRATIONS

CADET DAYS:

A STORY OF WEST POINT

CHAPTER I

"Pops, there's no use talking; we've simply got to send you to the Point."

"I'm sure I wish you could, Colonel. Father's tried every way he could think of, but cadetships don't go a-begging — out here, at least. The President has only one or two 'at large' appointments this year, and there were over a thousand applications for them."

"Well, have you tried Mr. Pierce, the Congressman for this district?"

"Oh, yes, sir, tried him long ago. He was very polite—Congressmen always are. He asked me to go round and get all the signatures to my application I possibly could, and kept me running for six weeks or so. Then he gave it to Mr. Breifogle's son."

Colonel Belknap smiled. "Yes, I remember
1

hearing," said he, reflectively, tapping his spurred boot-heel with his riding-switch and critically eying the sturdy young fellow who stood respectfully before him. George Graham, the post surgeon's eldest son, was just seventeen, of medium height, wiry and athletic in build, with deep chest and broad shoulders, with close-curling brown hair, with big, frank, steady blue eyes, and a complexion that was probably fair enough in his baby days, but now was so tanned by sun and wind that the down just sprouting on his cheeks and upper lip seemed almost white by contrast. A picture of boyish health, strength, and activity was "Geordie," as his mother ever called him in vain protest against the familiar " Pops " by which he was generally hailed—a pet name given him by the officers when he was but a " four-year-old," far out in Arizona—a boy who had been reared in the West, whose first playmate was a wild little Apache, whose earliest friends were the rough troopers at an isolated station ; a boy who had been taught to hunt and trail and shoot the Indian arrow before he was nine ; who had ridden " pony-back " across the continent from Arizona to Kansas with a cavalry column before he was ten ; who had stalked an antelope along the Smoky Hill before he was twelve ; who had shot a black bear in the Yellowstone Mountains when he was only fif-

teen; and raced a buffalo bull into the fords of
Milk River within sight of the British possessions
across latitude 49 within the following year. He
had met and mingled with Indians of many a
tribe. He had picked up something of the
Apache tongue from his playmate Dick; had visited the Navajo Reservation, near old Fort Defiance, in New Mexico, and brought away as his
very own one of their wonderful woven blankets.
He had learned not a little of the sign-language,
and so was able to communicate and make himself understood among even the Cheyenne ur-
chins around Fort Supply. After that his father
had been stationed just long enough at Niobrara
to enable Geordie to feel quite at home among
the Ogallala and Brulé Sioux, whose reservations
were just across the Dakota line, and whose visits to the post were frequent. Then the doctor
was ordered far up to Fort Assiniboine, where
Pops expected to freeze, but found the summer
days as hot as they were in Arizona, and the mos-
quitoes worse than they were at Supply. There
he studied the Northern Indians, and came to
the conclusion that the Blackfeet and Gros-Ven-
tres could not be compared favorably with the
lithe and sinewy and marvellously active Indians
of Arizona. Geordie swore by the Apaches.
There were no trailers like the Tontos; no bow-
men or ball-players like the Hualpais. The Sioux

and Cheyennes could ride, perhaps, but all the Sioux in Dakota could not whip Eskeldetsee's band "if you put 'em in the mountains"—which was probably true. And so by the time he was seventeen Geordie had ridden, marched, or travelled by ambulance, stage, or rail through most of the great Western States and Territories; but from the time he was four years old he had never been east of Omaha, or set foot in the streets of a bigger town than Cheyenne.

Nor had he ever regularly attended any school. There were no schools to speak of near any of the garrisons at which his father was stationed; but Dr. Graham was a man of scholarly tastes, a graduate of a famous university in Scotland, and one who by faithful study kept abreast of the leading minds in his profession. People generally led a very healthful open-air life on the broad Western frontier, and Dr. Graham had few patients to claim his time. He planned, therefore, all the studies for his two boys, he himself hearing them recite in history, geography, and arithmetic, while their devoted mother, at whose knee they had successively learned their A B C's, and whose fragile white hand had guided their chubby fists in the tracing of their first pothooks, was their instructor in the other rudiments.

Regularly, five mornings a week, the little fellows were set at their books right after guard-mounting, and, with brief intermission, worked until the bugles sounded "orderly call," or the drums and fifes merrily played "Roast Beef of Old England" at noon. No wonder they learned to welcome that call. Then they had their frugal luncheon. The doctor was a stanch Scotchman, who believed that boyish brawn and brain throve better on "parritch" and milk than on any other pabulum. Think of boys who never knew the taste of candy until after they were twelve—to whom hot biscuit was forbidden, and tea and coffee tabooed! They grew up ruddy-cheeked, freckle-faced, clear-eyed, sturdy-limbed, burly young "Hielanders," with marvellous capacity for solid food, sound sleep, and active sports. They were better taught than most of the other children around the garrisons, for what they knew they knew well. The three years' difference in their ages gave "Pops," of course, too much advantage in their boyish tiffs and scuffles; for boys will romp and wrestle, just as puppies play and kittens frolic, and these, starting in fun, close sometimes in fury; but they forget the feud as quickly as it was begun. Pops learned at an early age the lesson of self-restraint, the law of forbearance towards the younger and weaker brother. It was not learned intuitively, perhaps, but rather the reverse. The doctor was of a famous old Scotch Presbyterian clan, with a wholesome faith in Calvin and the doctrine of original sin. His gentle wife had thought to convert her eldest hope by appeals to his finer nature, but the doctor held that there was just so much of the "thrawn deevil" in every boy that had to be trounced out of him. It was all very well for Pops to tussle with his Apache playmate, and come home covered with dirt and bumps and glory, and explosive with tremendous tales of his personal valor — Pops would brag when he was young, and many another boy would have done the same under like conditions —but he was too big and strong for "Buddie;" and so when Bud came roaring in one day to tell how "Pops fwowed me down and hit me," Pops owned up that it was true. Bud *would* meddle with what he and Dick were trying to make, and he "just pushed him away." Mamma gravely admonished; but papa gave warning. It happened again before very long, and this time the doctor took Pops into his den, and presently poor Mrs. Graham ran to the dining-room and covered her ears, and Buddie howled in sudden revulsion of feeling. The doctor seldom punished, but what his right hand found to do he did with all his might.

"I want you to remember this, George," said he, half an hour later, "a manly boy must be merciful. It isn't enough that you should make allowances for Buddie's blunders, you must be lenient to his faults. When he is older he will be wiser. Meantime, the blows you strike must be for, not against him."

He needn't have said that. Pops was far readier to fight for his younger brother than he was to worry him in the least, and he took his flogging sorely to heart. He was only ten at the time. Bud had tried him severely. He had begged the little fellow to desist, and finally, losing all patience, had violated orders and thumped him—not very hard, perhaps, but still hard enough to warrant half at least of the pitiful tale the smaller boy ran to tell at once and at home. Geordie felt very much aggrieved at Bud when sent forth finally to go to his room and meditate on his sins and nurse his many sore spots; but when he saw the misery in the little fellow's face, when Bud, with fresh outburst of tears, threw himself into his brother's arms, clung to him sobbing, and could not say for the very violence of his grief how he hated himself for telling, the reconciliation was complete, and the three—mother and boys—stole away up-stairs and had a hug and cry together all by themselves, and came down again an hour later much happier after all, and quite ready to make it up with papa. But the doctor wasn't there. He had slipped out, despite the fact of its being his study hour, and was found at tea-time miserably promenading the bank of the stream half a mile from the post, and quite unconscious that the evening gun had fired. He never whipped Pops again; indeed, the boy gave him no cause to; and he never thrashed Buddie, even when that unrepentant little sinner well deserved it. He even declined to reprimand Pops at the excited appeal of Mrs. Captain Vaughan, whose twelve-year-old son came home from the swimming-pool, five days after, with a battered countenance, and a complaint that he had been beaten without cause by Pops Graham. Investigation of the case resulted in the fact that young Vaughan was trying to duck Buddie, when the latter's big brother happened upon the scene. Between the doctor and his boys there grew up a sort of tacit understanding, a firmly grounded trust and affection, that seldom found vent in caress of any kind, and was rarely apparent in word. George shot up from sturdy boyhood into athletic youth with thorough faith in his father, who, he believed, was the best friend he had or could expect to have. With all his heart he honored him, and with all his soul he loved his mother.

And now they were stationed at Fort Reynolds, with a thriving Western mining metropolis just six miles away to the east, with hunting and fishing in the lofty mountains to the west, and a great tumbling sea of grassy prairie stretching away to the east and south. Geordie's pony had been turned over to Bud long months ago, for the bigger boy could back and ride and control the liveliest bucker among all the bronchos in the cavalry stables. Officers and troopers alike declared that Pops was cut out for the cavalry. He loved a horse. He had broken and trained his last possession, a "cayuse" colt from the herd of old Two Moons, chief of the northern Cheyennes. He had ridden and hunted by himself, or with a single trooper for a companion, all through the mountains that frowned across the western sky, rarely coming home without an abundant supply of venison or bear meat, and still faithfully kept up his studies, hoping that by some good-fortune he might succeed in getting an appointment to the great Military Academy of the nation—hoping almost against hope, yet never desponding. At last it came, and this was the way of it.

Just as the wintry winds began to blow, and the soldiers, turning out for roll-call at the break of day, began to note how the mountains seemed to be wearing their fleecy nightcaps farther down about their ears until the bald peaks were covered with a glistening, spotless helmet, and the dark fringes of pine and fir down among the gorges and foot-hills looked all the blacker by contrast, there came a fresh battalion of cavalry marching into the post to relieve the ——th just ordered away, and Pops had sadly bidden adieu to the departing troops, little dreaming what warm friends he was destined to find among the new. First to arrive, with a single orderly in attendance, was the regimental quartermaster, Lieutenant Ralph McCrea, and to him said the quartermaster whom McCrea was to relieve:

"Mac, this young gentleman is Dr. Graham's son George, our candidate for West Point. He knows plainscraft, woodcraft, and mountain scouting as well as you do mathematics. He can ride as well as any man in my troop. Give him a lift in algebra and 'math.,' and he'll teach you all there is worth knowing about this part of the country."

The kindly young West-Pointer seemed to take at once to the surgeon's blushing boy. In the wintry weather that speedily set in there was little opportunity for hunting or exploration in the mountains; but in the long evenings McCrea became a frequent visitor at Dr. Graham's fireside, and finding that Pops had a sound analytical sort of brain in his curly pate, the quartermaster took delight in giving him stiff problems to work out, and taught him the West Point system of deducing rules instead of blindly following without knowing why or wherefore; and the friendship between them waxed and multiplied, and McCrea became warmly enlisted in the effort to secure a vacant cadetship for his boy friend. But knowing there was no chance "at large," as the President had already named his two candidates, the boy had done his best with the local Congressman, who, as Pops had said, had been most gracious and encouraging, but had bestowed the plum upon the son of his rich and influential constituent, Mr. Breifogle, whose brewery gave employment to over fifty voters. As alternate he had named the son of Counsellor Murphy, a lively local politician, and Pop's hopes were dashed.

Not so McCrea's. As quartermaster his duties called him frequently into town, where the First National Bank was the depository, and where he kept the large fund appropriated for rebuilding stables and quarters that had been destroyed by fire the previous year. "Neither of those young fellows," said he to Dr. Graham, "can pass the preliminary examination. It is by long odds too stiff for Breifogle mentally and for Murphy physically. Keep this to ourselves, and get Mr. Pierce to promise that George shall have the next vacancy. If we can get the Colonel to ask it, Pierce will say yes, perhaps; first because they served together in Virginia during the war, and second because he won't think he's promising anything at all. It's his first term, and he doesn't dream how hard that examination is, or how certain Breifogle is to fail. Now, if there were only some way we could 'get a pull' on him."

The way came sooner than was looked or hoped for. One December afternoon, just as the lights were peeping out here and there in the bustling shops of the busy Western town, and a thick, heavy cloud of snow was settling noiselessly upon roof and roadway, and all the foot-hills to the west were robed in white, and all the mountain passes deep in drifts, and the managers of the First National were congratulating themselves that their collections in the swarming mining settlements across the range were complete, and the thousands in coin and greenbacks safely hoarded in their vaults, and brewer Breifogle and two other opulent directors were seated with the president in the bank parlor, rubbing their hands over the neat balance exhibited, and discussing the propriety of a congratulatory despatch to Congressman Pierce, now at his post of duty at Washington, and the paying-teller had just completed the summing up of his cash account, and the bookkeeper was stowing away his huge volumes, and a clerk was lugging sacks of coin and stacks of Treasury notes into the open door of the vault, under the vigilant eye of the cashier, and the janitor had pulled down the shades and barred the iron shutters, and everything spoke eloquently of business security and prosperity—in stepped a squad of velvet-footed, soft-voiced, slouch-hatted strangers, and in the twinkling of an eye cashier and clerk, tellers, book-keeper, and janitor were as completely covered by six-shooters as the new-comers were with snow. It was a clear case of "hands up, everybody." Two of the party sidled into the parlor and stood guard over the magnates, three or four held the outer officials in statuesque discomfort, while two deft-handed individuals loaded up with bills and bags of gold, and vanished softly as they came. Their comrades gave them a start of sixty seconds, and then slowly and calmly backed out into the street, revolvers levelled to the last, and in less than four minutes from the moment of their entrance not one of the gang was in sight. Timing their arrival exactly, they had ridden into town from the northwest just at dusk, left their strong, spirited horses, held by accomplices in a side street not fifty yards away ; were in and out, up and away again, in less time than it takes to tell it, and with them ninety thousand dollars in cash.

Vain the rush of clerks and tellers and directors into the snow-covered street. Vain the yells of "Murder!" "Robbers!" "Road-agents!" A crowd collected in a few minutes, but all were afoot and powerless to follow. It would be an hour before the sheriff could muster a mounted party strong enough to pursue; but he had his wits about him.

"It's the old Hatton gang, sure!" he cried. "They dare not go to the mines. They'll make for Marcy's Pass, and scatter when they get to the cove beyond. There's only one hope." And like a deer the active frontiersman ran to the telegraph office.

"Rush this out to the fort!" he cried, as he pencilled a despatch.

"First National just robbed by Hatton gang. Ten men. Ninety thousand gone. Government funds mostly. ["That 'll make him act," he muttered.] They're making for Marcy's Pass. You can head 'em off by Squaw Cañon if you send cavalry at once. We follow trail. Answer.

"BRENT, Sheriff."

Colonel Belknap, with a knot of officers, was in the club-room just after stables when the despatch was handed to him by the breathless operator. He was an old campaigner, who had served almost a lifetime in the West.

"Mount your troop instantly, Lane!" he called to one of his most trusted captains. "Never mind their supper; they can have that later. Listen to this." And he read the despatch aloud.

The entrance to Marcy's Pass lay about nine miles nearly due west from town. Hatch's Cove was a lovely nook in the summer - time, but almost inaccessible in winter, lying across the range, and approached from the east by the old road through the Pass. Lance Creek, a clear and beautiful stream, rose in the cove and made its way through the range by means of a tortuous and wellnigh impassable gorge known as Squaw Cañon, which opened into the foot-hills not more than two miles and a half away to the westward of Fort Reynolds. All this was promptly discussed even as the sergeants' voices could be heard ringing out the order in the barrack corridors across the parade.

"Turn out, 'E' troop, lively; carbines and revolvers, fur coats and gloves. Jump now, men!"

Down went knife and fork, cup and spoon. Up sprang the laughing, chaffing, boisterous crowd of the moment before. Away they tore to their bunk-room, and grabbed their great-coats and furs; away to the arm-racks for carbine and six - shooter. Quickly they buckled the broad woven cartridge - belts, and then went bounding down the barrack stairs, forming ranks in the softly falling snow. Double time they trotted down to the long, dimly lighted stables, and in among their astonished and snorting horses. In ten minutes they were trotting away to the westward through wellnigh impenetrable darkness, through a muffling snowfall, over an unseen and unknown trail, yet hesitating not a minute; trotting buoyantly, confidently ahead, following a guide who knew every inch of the way to and through the cañon and miles and miles beyond.

"Who can lead them? What scouts have you on your roll who know the hills?" was the Colonel's anxious query of his quartermaster, while the troop was saddling.

"No scouts left, sir, now; but we don't need them. Here's Geordie Graham."

Yes, Pops, and the doctor too, both in saddle and ready; so was McCrea, and so it happened that less than an hour later Luke and Jim Hatton, leaders of the band, bearers of most of the spoil, a hundred yards ahead of their fellows as they issued from the westward end of Marcy's Pass, deeming themselves perfectly secure from any capture except from the rear, ten safe miles away from town, rode slap in among a whole troop of cavalry, and were knocked on the head, disarmed, dismounted, and relieved of their plunder before they could fire a shot or utter a cry of warning.

"FOLLOWING A GUIDE WHO KNEW EVERY INCH OF THE WAY"

"We never could have got them in all the world, sir," said both Lane and McCrea, " but for Pops here. He knew the way, even in the dark, and we headed them off in the nick of time."

It was this service that called forth Colonel Belknap's remarks at the head of this chapter. It was this that prompted him to say to the officers of the First National next day that the least they could do was to telegraph the Honorable Mr. Pierce, M.C., urging him to promise that the next vacancy at West Point should be filled by George Montrose Graham. It was the despatch signed by these officials and a dozen leading citizens—for McCrea struck while the iron was hot, and took the paper around himself— that caused Mr. Pierce to wire his pledge in reply. And one day in February there came a note to Dr. Graham's, saying that Counsellor Murphy had been convinced by the leading medical practitioner in town that his boy could never pass the physical examination at the Point, and would better be turning his talents to some other channel, and then Colonel Belknap reminded Mr. Pierce of his promise, and Pierce was caught. On Valentine's Day in 188–, to Geordie Graham's speechless joy and Buddie's enthusiastic delight, a big official envelope of the War Department was placed in the former's hand. He knew what it meant. He went over and threw his arms around his mother's neck and bent and kissed her, for her loving eyes were swimming in tears.

CHAPTER II

AMONG the formal official documents in the envelope which brought such delight to the Graham family was one giving in detail the qualifications necessary to secure the admission of a candidate to West Point. He was subjected soon after his arrival, so said the papers, to a rigid physical examination by a board of experienced surgeons. Glancing over the array of causes of disqualification, it was apparent to the doctor that an absolutely perfect physique was necessary, but on all these points he felt well assured. As to other qualifications, the age for admission of cadets to the Academy was stated to be between seventeen and twenty-two years. Candidates must be unmarried, at least five feet in height, free from any infectious or immoral disorder, and generally from any deformity, disease, or infirmity which might in the faintest degree render them unfit for military service. They must be well versed in reading, in writing, including orthography, in arithmetic, and have a knowledge of the elements of English grammar, of descriptive geography, particularly of our own country, and of the history of the United States. That seemed simple enough. On all these points Geordie, as well as his father, had no doubt whatever. "Sound as a dollar" was the universal verdict, and the wisdom of his father's rigid system of training was all the more apparent. But when they came to look over the formidable list of specimens of the problems and questions which the candidates were required to solve and answer, the boy's heart failed him a little. Even McCrea shook his head over some of them.

"It is ten years since I went up for my examination, just as you are to go, Pops—an army boy who had had precious little schooling; but I don't remember any problems as hard as this one." And the Quartermaster wrinkled his brows over a complicated example, while Captain Lane, poring over a big atlas, was hunting for a chain of mountains he could not remember ever before having heard of.

"It seems a queer confession," said the latter, "but I don't believe I could begin to pass the entrance examination to the Academy, from which I was graduated so many years ago. I certainly couldn't without months of preparation."

The Colonel suggested that perhaps these hard nuts were ladled out in order to stimulate the candidate to closer study. The questions really propounded would not be so difficult. But the doctor and McCrea were determined to take no chances.

"There are only three months left for preparation," said Graham; "the question is how to employ the time to best advantage. George is willing to study hard, and you and I to teach, but what I'm thinking is that we may be wasting time on immaterial points and neglecting some that are essential. Would it not be best to send him on and have him study under some one who knows just exactly what is needed?"

And McCrea said, "Yes," and wrote forthwith to an old friend, an officer whom severe wounds had incapacitated for active service, and who had opened a school of preparation at the Point adapted to the needs of candidates for admission. And so it resulted that early in April, for the first time in his life, Geordie Graham was to leave father, mother, and Bud, and, for the first time since he was a mere baby-boy, to set foot across the Missouri.

Over that farewell we need not linger. How many big, salty tears were dropped into the depths of the trunk no one on earth but the loving mother who packed it could ever tell. Yet even now, face to face with the inevitable separation, not one word would she say that might cast a shadow over the hopes of her big boy, as she spoke of Geordie as a means of distinguishing him from Bud, her "little Benjamin." Fondly had she hoped that as he grew older Geordie's tastes would turn to some other profession, but she hoped in vain. First, last, and all the time, ever since the troopers at Verde decorated him with his Corporal's chevrons when he was a mite of a four-year-old, the longing of his heart was to be a soldier. For boys with that ambition there is no school like West Point; for boys without it, any other school would be better.

"There isn't a man in all 'E' troop that isn't sorry to have you leave the fort, Geordie," said old Sergeant Nolan, as the boy went the rounds at afternoon stables, bidding his friends good-bye, and taking a farewell look at his favorite horses; "but what's more, sir," he added, with a respectful touch of the cap visor as Captain Lane appeared, "there isn't a man but that's glad he's going to West Point, and that wouldn't like to see him with us again as our Lieutenant."

"But I'm not in yet, Sergeant," laughed Geordie. "There is Mr. Breifogle to be considered. If he passes, there'll be no room for me; and if he fails, why, I may too. In that event, I'll have to come back and 'list just as soon as I'm eighteen."

And yet Geordie felt no such misgiving as he sat silently in the dark corner of the ambulance, choking down some troublesome lumps that had risen in his throat, and made his eyes blind as his mother's arms were unclasped about his neck. The principal of the school which young Breifogle had been attending for two years had told Mr. McCrea that the boy was neither apt nor studious, that he had twice failed in his examinations for promotion to higher grade, and that only after infinite pains and much help had he been able to answer the sample questions enclosed with his letter of appointment. When asked why old Mr. Breifogle did not withdraw his son from a race in which he had no chance, the master laughed.

"Breifogle is like a great many of our people who have become suddenly rich," said he. " He thinks money and a political pull will do anything. He refuses to believe that West Point is governed by rules that even the President cannot violate. He is confident that all that is necessary is for him to go on with Fritz in June, and the examiners will not dare reject him, especially if Congressman Pierce is there, too."

Now this was no exaggeration. Mr. Breifogle really thought it a very unjustifiable thing in an army officer, supporting a family on so small a salary, to undergo the expense of sending George all the way to West Point and back, for back he felt sure he would have to come. It was still worse to send him ahead of time and pay board and school bills. He and Fritz would not go until June.

"I'm really sorry for the old fellow," said McCrea; "he's so thoroughly earnest and honest in his convictions. It isn't his fault, either. It is part of the stock in trade of many politicians to make their constituents believe that for the benefit of their special friends they have it in their power to set aside laws, rules, or regulations. I haven't a doubt that Pierce has made the old man believe he 'stands' in with the Secretary of War and the Superintendent of the Academy, and that Fritz will go through West Point with flying colors. It will cost Breifogle nearly a thousand dollars to find out his mistake."

This was several years ago, it must be remembered, in the days when all candidates were required to present themselves for examination at the Point instead of appearing before boards of army officers at convenient garrisons throughout the country, as is the case to-day.

"No, Geordie, my boy," said McCrea, in conclusion, "I don't like to take comfort in another man's misfortunes, but there is no chance whatever for young Breifogle and every chance for you. All you have to do is study and you'll win. I have said as much to the old man, for he stopped me at the bank the other day and asked what I thought of the case, and I told him frankly. For a moment he looked downcast; then he brightened up all of a sudden, laid his finger alongside his nose, and winked at me profoundly. ' Vell, you yust vait a leetle,' he said, and turned away. I've no doubt he thinks I'm only trying to bluff him out in your interest."

Two days more, and George, standing on the rear platform of the Pullman, looking down with no little awe upon the swollen, turbid, ice-whirling waters of the Missouri, far beneath the splendid spans of the great railway bridge. Another day, and his train seemed to be rolling through miles of city streets and squares before it was finally brought to a stand under the grimy roof of the station at Chicago. Here from the windows of the rattling omnibus that bore him across the town to the depot of the Michigan Central he gazed in wonderment at the height of the buildings on every side. Early the next morning he was up and dressed, and just before sunrise stepped out on the wooden staging at Falls View, listening to the voice and seeing for the first time the beauty and grandeur of Niagara. A few minutes later, looking from the car window, he seemed to be sailing in mid-air over some tremendous gorge, in whose depths a broad torrent of deep green water, flecked with foam and tossing huge crunching masses of ice, went roaring away beneath him. *Such* a letter as he wrote to mother that morning, as hour after hour he sped along eastward over bands of glistening steel, flying like the wind, yet so smoothly that his pen hardly shook. Think what a revelation it must have been to that frontier-bred boy, whose whole life had been spent among the mountains or prairies of the Far West, to ride all the morning long through one great city after another, through the heart of Buffalo, Rochester, Syracuse, Utica, and Albany. The Mohawk Valley seemed one long village to him, so unaccustomed were his eyes to country thickly settled. The Hudson, still fettered with ice above the railway bridge and just opening below, set his heart to beating, for now West Point lay but a hundred miles away. How the train seemed to whiz along those bold, beautiful shores, undulating at first, but soon becoming precipitous and rocky! Many people gazed from the westward windows at the snow-covered Catskills as the afternoon began to wane; but Geordie had seen mountains beside which these were but hillocks. The clustering towns, the frequent rush of engines and cars, the ever-increasing bustle, however, impressed him greatly. Every now and then his train fairly shot past stations where crowds of people stood waiting.

"Didn't they want to get on?" he asked the Pullman porter.

"Oh yes, sir, wanted to bad 'nough; but, Lord bless you, dis train don't stop for them: they has to wait for the locals. We runs a hundred trains a day along here. Dis train don't even stop where you gets off, sir; that's why you have to change at Poughkeepsie, the only place we stop between Albany and New York."

Surely enough, they rolled in presently under lofty bluffs under a bridge so high in the air that its trusses looked like a spider-web, and then stopped at a station thronged with people; and Pops, feeling not a little bewildered, found himself standing with his hand luggage, looking blankly after the car that had borne him so comfortably all the way from Chicago, and now disappeared in the black depths of the stone-faced tunnel to the south, seeming to contract like a leaking balloon as it sped away. Hardly was it out of sight when another train slid in to replace it, and everybody began tumbling aboard.

"This for Garrisons?" he asked a bearded official in blue and brass buttons.

A nod was the answer. Railway men are too busy to speak; and Pops followed the crowd, and took a seat on the river-side. The sun was well down to the westward now; the Hudson grew broader, blacker, and deeper at every turn;

the opposite shores cast longer shadows; the electric lights were beginning to twinkle across the wide reach at Newburg; then a rocky islet stood sentinel half-way across to a huge rounded rock-ribbed height. The train rushed madly into another black tunnel, and came tearing forth at the southern end, and Pops's heart fairly bounded in his breast. Lo! there across the deep narrow channel towered Crow's Nest and Storm King. This was the heart of the Highlands. Never before had he seen them, yet knew them at a glance. What hours had he not spent over the photograph albums of the young graduates? Another rush through rocky cuts, and then a smooth, swift spin around a long, gradual curve, lapped by the waters of the Hudson, and there, right before his eyes, still streaked with snow, was West Point, the flag just fluttering from its lofty staff at the summons of the sunset gun.

Ten minutes later and the ferry-boat was paddling him across the river, almost the only passenger. The hush of twilight had fallen. The Highlands looked bare and brown and cheerless in their wintry guise. Far away to the south the crags of Dunderberg were reverberating with the roar of the train as it shot through Anthony's Nose. The stars were just beginning to peep out here and there in the eastern sky, and a pallid crescent moon hung over against them in the

west. All else was dark and bleak. The spell
of the saddest hour of the day seemed to chill
the boy's brave heart, and for the first time a
homesick longing crept over him. This was the
cheery hour at the army fireside, far out among
the Rockies—the hour when they gathered about
the open hearth and heaped on the logs, and
mother played soft, sweet melodies at the piano,
often the songs of Scotland, so dear to them all.
Pops couldn't help it; he was beginning to feel
a little blue and cold and hungry. One or two
passengers scurried ashore and clambered into
the yellow omnibus, waiting there at the dock as
the boat was made fast in her slip.

"Where do you go?" asked the driver of the
boy.

"Send my trunk up to the hotel," said Geordie,
briefly. "I'm going to walk."

They had figured it all out together before he
started from home, he and Mr. McCrea. "The
battalion will be coming in from parade as you
reach the Point, Geordie, if your train's on time."
And the boy had determined to test his knowledge of topography as learned from the maps he
had so faithfully studied. Slinging his bag into
the 'bus, he strode briskly away, crossed the
tracks of the West Shore Road, turned abruptly
to his right, and breasted the long ascent, the
stage toiling behind him. A few minutes' uphill

walk, and the road turned to the left near the top of the bluff. Before him, on the north, was the long gray massive façade of the riding-hall; before him, westward, another climb, where, quitting the road, he followed a foot-path up the steep and smoothly rounded terrace, and found himself suddenly within stone's-throw of the very buildings he sought. At the crest of the gentle slope to the north, the library with its triple towers; to its left, the solid little chapel; close at hand to his right front, the fine headquarters' building; beyond that, dim and indistinct, the huge bulk of the old academic building; and directly ahead of him, its great windows brilliantly lighted, a handsome gray stone edifice, with its arched doorway and broad flight of steps in the centre—the cadet mess-hall, as it used to be termed, the Grant Hall of to-day. His pulses throbbed as he stepped across the road and stood on the flag-stones beneath the trees. A sentry sauntering along the walk glanced at him keenly, but passed him by without a word.

Suddenly there rose on the still evening air the tramp of coming soldiery, quick and alert, louder and louder, swifter than the bounding of his heart and far more regular. Suddenly through the broad space between the academic and the north end of the mess-hall, straight as a ruler, came the foremost subdivision, the first platoon

"A SENTRY GLANCED AT HIM KEENLY"

of Company A, and instantly in response to the ringing order, "Column right," from some deep manly voice farther towards the rear, the young cadet officer in front whirled about and ordered "Right wheel." Another second and around swept the perfect line in the heavy gray over-coats, the little blue forage-caps pulled well down over the smooth-shaved, grave, yet youthful faces dimly seen under the gaslight. Then on they swept, platoon after platoon, in strong double rank, each in succession wheeling again steadily to the right as it reached the broad flight of steps, then breaking and bounding lightly to the top, every man for himself, until, one after the other, each of the eight subdivisions was swallowed up in the great hall, echoing for a moment with chat and laughter, the rattle of chairs, the clatter of knife and fork and spoon, and then the big doors swung to, and Pops, for the first time in his life, had seen the famous battalion which it was his most ardent wish to join. For a moment he stood there silent, his heart still beating high, then with one long sigh of mingled envy and gratification he turned away.

That same evening, wasting no time after he had eaten a hearty supper at Craney's, Geordie sought and found Lieutenant B——. Everything had been arranged by letter; his coming was ex-pected, and in a few moments the boy and his instructor were seated in a quiet room, and Pops's preliminary examination was really begun. In less than an hour Mr. B—— had decided pretty thoroughly where his instruction was already satisfactory and where it was incomplete.

"There's no question as to your physique, Mr. Graham," said the Lieutenant, smiling to see the blush of shy delight with which the boy welcomed the first use of the "handle" to his name. Hitherto he had been Geordie or Pops to everybody. "I fancy it won't take long to make you more at home in mathematics. To-morrow we'll move you into your temporary quarters down at the Falls, and next day begin studies. There are several candidates on the ground already."

And so within the week our young plainsman was practically in harness, and with a dozen other aspirants trudging twice a day over the mile of road connecting the Point and the village below; studying hard, writing home regularly, hearing a great deal of information as to the antecedents and expectations of most of his new associates, but partly from native reticence and partly from due regard of McCrea's cautions, saying little as to his past experiences, and nothing at all as to his hopes for the future. "No matter what you do know of actual service, Pops —and you have had more experience of army life than ninety-nine per cent. of the corps—it is best not to 'let on' that you know anything until you are an old cadet, even among your classmates."

Some of his new associates Pops found congenial, some antagonistic; but the one thing he kept in mind was that all were merely conditional. Not until after the June examination would they really know who were and who were not to be of "the elect." "Those who are most volubly confident to-day," wrote McCrea, "are the ones who will be most apt to fail. Keep your own counsel, 'give every man thine ear and few thy voice'—and that's all."

George had some novel experiences in those days of preparation, and met some odd characters among the boys, but as few of these had any bearing on his subsequent history they need not be dwelt upon. With only one did he strike up anything approximating an intimacy, and that was after the first of May and was unavoidable, because the young fellow became his room-mate, for one thing, and was so jolly, cheery, confident, and enthusiastic, for another, that Graham simply couldn't help it.

Along in May his letters had a good deal to say about Mr. Frazier, and by June the Falls began to fill up with young fellows from all over the country. By this time the daily sight of the battalion at its drills and parades was perfectly

familiar to those on the ground, and yet the gulf
between cadets and candidates seemed utterly
unbridgable.   Dr. Graham had thought it a.
good thing for Geordie to go with letters of in-
troduction from Colonel Fellows, of Fort Union,
to his son, a Second Class man, or from Major
Freeland, of Bridger, whose boy was in the Third,
but McCrea said: "No; there is just one way
to win the respect and good-will of the corps of
cadets," he declared, "and all the letters and all
the fathers and uncles and even pretty sisters
combined can't win it any other way. The boy
must earn it himself, and it isn't to be earned in
a month, either. Every tub stands on its own
bottom there, doctor. The higher a fellow's con-
nections, the more he has to be taken down.
Leastwise, it was so in my time, and West Point
is deteriorating if it is any different now."

Strange, therefore, as it may seem, though he
knew many a cadet by sight and name, not one
had George Graham become acquainted with until the momentous 15th of June, when, with a
number of other young civilians, he reported
himself in a room in the eighth division of barracks to Cadet Lieutenant Merrick; was turned
over to Cadet Corporal Stone to be taken to the
hospital for physical examination, and in one of
the surgeons recognized an old friend of his father's whom he knew in Arizona, but who appar-

ently didn't know Geordie from Adam. One hundred and forty-seven young fellows entered the hospital hopefully that day, and among these over twenty-five were rejected. Among those who passed was Breifogle. The old gentleman himself was on hand in front of the mess-hall, when next morning those who had passed the scrutiny of the surgeons were marshalled thither to undergo the written examination in arithmetic.

Promptly, under the eye of the Professor of Mathematics, a number of young officers assigned the candidates to seats and set them at their tasks. Geordie felt that his face was very white, but he strove to think of nothing but the work in hand. Slowly he read over the twelve problems on the printed page, then, carefully and methodically, began their solution. Long, long before he was through he saw Frazier rise and, with confident, almost careless mien, hand his complete work to the secretary, and saunter out into the sunshine. Long before he had finished he saw many another go, less jauntily, perhaps, but with quiet confidence.

One by one most of Mr. B——'s pupils finished inside the allotted two hours and a half; but Geordie, with the thoroughness of his race, again and again went over his work before he was satisfied he, at least, could not improve it. Then he arose, and trembling a bit despite himself, handed his paper to the silent officer. A number, fully twenty, were still seated, some of them helplessly biting their pencils and looking furtively and hopelessly about them. One of these was Fritz Breifogle, for whom the old gentleman was still waiting on the walk outside. Some officers, noticing the father's anxiety, had kindly invited him into the mess-parlor, and had striven to comfort him with cooling drink and a cigar. He was grateful, but unhappy. Already it had begun to dawn upon him that what he had been told of West Point was actually true: neither money nor influence could avail, and Fritz was still at his fruitless task when "the hammer fell."

Another day and the suspense was over. A score more of the young fellows, who were still faintly hopeful at dinner-time, were missing at the next muster of the candidates at retreat. Breifogle was gone without a word to his alternate. The way was clear at last, and, more madly than ever, Pops's heart bounded in his breast as in stern official tone Cadet Corporal Loring read rapidly the alphabetical list of the successful candidates—George Montrose Graham among them.

CHAPTER III

AND now, with examinations over, and no remaining doubts or fears, there was probably no happier boy in all the " menagerie " than Geordie Graham. As for the hundred young fellows in civilian dress, " herded " three and four in each room, and wrestling with their first experiences of cadet life, it is safe to say most of the number were either homesick or in some way forlorn. Nothing so utterly destroys the glamour that hovers over one's ideas of West Point as the realities of the first fortnight. Of his three roommates *pro tempore*, Bennie Frazier had already announced time and again that if a beneficent Creator would forgive him the blunder of coming here at all, he'd square accounts by quitting as quick as he possibly could. Winn, a tall Kentuckian, wanted to resign, but was too plucky. Connell, a bulky young Badger, had written two terrific screeds to his uncle, the member from Pecatonica, denouncing the cadet officials as brutes, bullies, and tyrants, which documents were duly forwarded with appropriate complaint to the War Department, and formed the text for a furious leader in the *Pecatonica Pilot*, clamoring for the abolition of West Point. The letters were duly referred to the Superintendent United States Military Academy for remark, and by him to the commandant of cadets, by which time Mr. Connell was a duly accredited high private in the rear rank of Company B, and had almost forgotten the woes of early barrack days, and was not a little abashed and dismayed when summoned before the grave, dignified Colonel to make good his allegations. It took him just ten seconds to transfer any lingering resentment for the cadet corporals to the avuncular M. C., whom with boyish inconsistency he now berated for being such a fool as to make a fuss about a little thing like that. Among the new cadets were a very few who, as sons of army officers, knew perfectly well what they had to expect. These and a number of young fellows who, like Graham, had come on months or weeks beforehand and placed themselves under tuition, were well prepared for the ordeal of the entrance examinations as well as for other ordeals which followed.

Even among them, however, were many who looked upon life with eyes of gloom. The ceaseless routine of drill, drill, of sharp reprimand, of stern, unbending discipline, wofully preyed upon their spirits. Their hearts were as sore as their unaccustomed muscles. But with Pops all was different. He had reached at last the goal of his ambition. He had won his way through many a discouragement to the prize of a cadetship. Now he was ready, even eager, to be tried and tested in every way, to show his grit, and to prove his fitness for the four years' race for the highest prize of all, the diploma and commission. The drill that made his comrades' muscles ache was a bagatelle to him. From earliest boyhood he had watched the recruits at setting-up, and not only learned and practised all, but with Bud and Dick for his squad would often convulse the officers at Verde and Supply by his imitation of Sergeant Feeny's savage Hibernian manner. The cadet yearling who was drill-master of the four to which Pops was assigned saw at once that he had a "plebe corporal"—a young fellow who had been pretty well drilled—and all the more did he rasp him when anything went amiss. Many of the new-comers had been through squad-drill at military schools or in cadet companies, but never under such rigid, relentless discipline as this. Every cadet drill-master carried the steel rammer of his rifle as a drill-stick, and was just about as unbending as his rod of office. Poor Frazier was in hot-water all the time—as well as in the sulks.

"I belonged to the high-school cadets for two

years, and everybody that ever saw us drill said we could lay over anything in the whole country," he protested, "and now here's this measly little stuck-up prig, that probably never knew anything about drill until he entered here last year, correcting and finding fault with everything I do. I ain't going to stand it, by thunder! I've written to my father to come on again, and just have this thing attended to right off." And Frazier's handsome boyish face was flushed with wrath, and clouded with a sense of wrong and indignity. "It seems to me if I were in your place I wouldn't stand being abused either, Graham. I heard Mr. Flint snapping at you again this morning."

Pops was busily engaged dusting for the tenth time the iron mantel-shelf and the little looking-glass. He half turned. "Wa-e-l," he said, while a grin of amusement hovered about the corners of his mouth, "Flint was all right, I guess. Your squad was just in front of us, and when I saw Connell stumble over your heels and try to climb up your back, I laughed out loud. He caught me chuckling."

"Yes, and abused you like a pick-pocket, by jingo! If my father were an officer in the regular army, as yours is, it wouldn't happen twice to me."

"No, nor to me either," chimed in Connell.

THE AWKWARD SQUAD

"I'll bet you he'd sing a mighty different tune if he knew you were the son of a Major."

"Well, there's just where you're 'way off," answered Geordie, after the manner of the frontier. "Of all places in creation this is the one where one's dad cuts no figure whatever. I've often heard old officers say that the boys who got plagued and tormented most in their time were the fellows whose fathers were generals or cabinet ministers. Fred Grant wouldn't have had half as hard a time if his father hadn't been President. Frazier's whole trouble comes from letting on that he knew all about drill before he got here; that's the truth of it. I get along smoothly by pretending never to have known anything."

"Oh, a lot you have! If that snob Loring ever speaks to me as he spoke to you this morning about laughing in the ranks, I'll—I'll just let him have my fist between the eyes, and he'll see more stars than he ever saw before, if he is a color corporal. What 'll your father say when he hears that he threatened to put you in a cell just for laughing when that Pike County fellow knocked his hat off trying to salute?"

"Well, he didn't say cell, in the first place, and father wouldn't hear it from me, at least, if he had. It's an understood thing at home that they're to ask no questions, and I'm to tell no tales until plebe camp is over and done with. Plebes don't begin to have the hard times now that they had thirty years ago, and if they could stand it then, I can now. All you've got to do is simply make up your mind to grin and bear it; do just as you're told, and say nothing about it. If this thing worries you now, when only our drill-masters and instructors get at us, what are you going to do, Frazier, when you're marched over there into camp next week and turned over to the tender mercies of the whole corps?"

"I'm going to fight the first man that offers me an indignity of any kind, by thunder!"

Geordie burst into one of his merry laughs, just as a light foot came bounding up the iron stairway. Bang! A single knock at the door. Up sprang the four boys, heels and knees together, heads up, eyes straight to the front, arms and hands braced against the sides, the palms of the latter turned outward as far as the youngsters could force them and thereby work their shoulders back, each young fellow facing the centre of the bare and cheerless room. Enter Cadet Corporal Loring, his jaunty gray coat fitting like wax, not a crease nor a wrinkle anywhere, every one of his three rows of bell buttons glistening, his gold chevrons gleaming, his white collar, cuffs, gloves, and trousers simply immaculate, everything so trig and military, all in such wondrous contrast to the sombre garb of the four plebes. His clear-cut face is stern and dignified.

"What is the meaning of all this noise?" he asks. "Who was laughing as I came in?"

"I was, sir," promptly answers Graham.

"You again, Mr. Graham? This is the third time since reveille I've had to reprimand you for chuckling like a school-boy—twice in ranks, and now again at inspection. What were you laughing at this time, sir?" inquired Mr. Loring, majestically.

"At something Frazier said, sir."

"*Mr.* Frazier, sir. Never omit the handle to a gentleman's name on duty or in official intercourse. Only among yourselves and off duty can you indulge in familiarity; *never*, sir, in conversation with superior officers." (Oh, the immensity of distance between the plebe and the yearling corporal!) "And you are room orderly, too, Mr. Graham, and responsible for the appearance of things. Where should the broom be, sir?"

"Behind the door, sir."

"Then where is it, sir?"

And for the first time poor Pops sees that in the heat of argument, Frazier, dusting off his shoes with that implement, had left it across the room in the alcove. Still, it was his own business to see that it was in place, so he had nothing to say beyond, "I didn't notice it until just now, sir."

"Exactly, Mr. Graham; if you had been attending to your duty instead of giggling over Mr. Frazier's witticisms you would have escaped punishment. Report at my office immediately after supper this evening, sir." And then, after finding perhaps a pin-head of dust behind the looking-glass, and further rebuking Mr. Graham for unmilitary carelessness, the young gentleman proceeds to carry dismay into the next room.

And that evening, after supper, as ordered, Pops tapped at the awful door, was bidden to enter and listen to his doom. Cadet Lieutenant Merrick sat in judgment. For levity in ranks, dust on mantel, broom out of place at inspection, new Cadet Graham was directed to walk post in the hall until drum-beat at tattoo.

Outside the door, standing meekly in the hallway, awaiting summons to enter, were half a dozen of his comrades, about to be sentenced to similar punishment for blunders of greater or less magnitude. Some looked woe-begone, some foolish, some were laughing, but all assumed the required expression of gravity as Mr. Loring came forth with his victim. In two minutes our Geordie found himself slowly pacing the hallway on the second floor, with strict orders to keep his little fingers on the seams of his trousers, the palms of his hands to the front, and to hold conversation with nobody except in the line of duty. For a moment he could not but feel a little wrathful and disheartened, but again McCrea's words came to his aid: "Remember that the first thing that will be sorely tested is your sense of subordination—your readiness to obey without question. No soldier is considered fit to command others until he can command himself. They purposely put a fellow through all manner of predicament just to test his grit. Don't let anything ruffle your temper, and they will soon find you need no lessons." And so, like a sentry, he patiently tramped his post, listening to the music of the band at an evening concert out on the Plain, and keeping watchful eye for the coming of cadet officials. Along towards nine o'clock up came Cadet Lieutenant Merrick, commanding the plebes; and "Pops," as he had been taught, halted, faced him, and stood attention.

"Why are you on punishment to-night, sir?" was the question.

Pops colored, but answered promptly, "Laughing in ranks, broom out of place, and some other things, sir."

"Yes, I remember. Go to your quarters now, and keep your face straight on duty hereafter."

Involuntarily Geordie raised his hand in salute, as for years he had seen the soldiers do after receiving orders from an officer, then turned to go.

"One moment, Mr. Graham. Whose squad are you in?"

"Mr. Flint's, sir."

"Did he teach you that salute?"

"No, sir," stammered Geordie.

"Where did you learn it?"

"Among the soldiers, sir, in the garrison."

"Ah, yes, I've heard of your case. That 'll do, sir."

Back in his room Pops found his three comrades in excited discussion. Something tremendous had happened. While Geordie, obedient to his orders, had gone to report to the cadet officer, Frazier, exulting in his knowledge of the Point, had persuaded Connell to trust himself to his guidance and go out for a walk. For half an hour after returning from supper the new cadets were allowed release from quarters, and permitted to visit each other and stroll about the grounds as they might see fit, but were cautioned not to venture over towards camp. The Graduating Class had now been gone, with the happy furloughmen, an entire week. The rest of the corps, the new First and Third Classes, had marched into their summer quarters over across the cavalry plain, among the beautiful trees south of old Fort Clinton. The new cadets, still in the garb of

civil life, were "herded together," as the old cadets expressed it, at the barracks, and thither the older cadets now were forbidden to go. Except in the mess-hall, three times a day, they were seen, therefore, only by their barrack instructors and their squad drill-masters. As a result of this plan the wholesale system of hazing, plaguing, and tormenting that prevailed at the Point some thirty years ago was wellnigh prevented. Not so, however, the impulse. Just so long as human nature remains as it is and has been since creation, "boys will be boys," and rare indeed are the boy-natures which know not the longing to play tricks upon new-comers, especially at school or college. Even among mature men the impulse lingers. Added, therefore, to the line of demarcation mentioned in the interest of discipline between the plebe and the upper-class man there ever exists the temptation to have sport at the expense of the new-comers, and only by most stringent measures has the spirit been controlled to the extent that it is.

So long as Geordie and his comrades kept to the neighborhood of the barracks, however, they were safe. A few of their number had been run up into the rooms of the yearlings the day before camp, where they were instantly surrounded by a frantic mob of young fellows mad with exultation at being at last released from plebehood, and eager to try on the new boys the experiments lavished on them a twelvemonth previous. The officer in charge caught sound of the affair, however, and made instant descent upon the division, only, of course, to find the suspected room deserted, and all the others crowded by old cadets, and the only faces that looked in the faintest degree conscious of guilt or wrong were those of the luckless plebes themselves, who, cautioned against entering the barracks of the elders, were nevertheless caught in the act, and could never explain any more than they could help their presence on dangerous and forbidden ground.

Benny Frazier was loud in his ridicule of Winn, who was one of the party entrapped. No yearling and no squad or party of yearlings could get him where he didn't mean or wish to go, he frequently said; and for no other reason than that he had been officially warned to keep away from camp had Benny become possessed with the longing to cruise thither. Old cadets couldn't cross sentry posts and nab them, he argued. "We'll just aggravate them by coming so near, and yet keeping aloof." Poor, crestfallen, indignant Benny! He and Connell had sallied forth, had gone strolling over the plain and along the south side of camp, between the field battery and the tents, had smilingly declined the eager invitation of the yearlings, who crowded down along the post of the sentry on Number Five, urging them to enter and make themselves at home. In the consciousness of his superior wisdom Benny had even ventured upon an expressive gesture with his thumb at the tip of his nose, his fingers wiggling in air. Poor boy! There were instant and stentorian shouts for the corporal of the guard. Down at a run from the guard-tent came a patrol. Eager hands pointed the way; eager voices clamored for their arrest. Benny and Connell were surrounded in an instant. Glistening bayonets were levelled at their throbbing hearts. "March!" was the order, and amid the jeers and rejoicing of a hundred young scamps in gray and white the two poor plebes were sternly marshalled to the guard-tents, and into the awful presence of the cadet officer of the day, charged with having disobeyed the sentinel's order not to pass between the guns, and, far worse, of having made insulting gestures to a sentry in the solemn discharge of his duty. It was an impressive moment. There stood the stern young cadet captain in his tall plume and crimson sash and gold-laced sleeves, astounded at the effrontery of these young yet hardened reprobates.

"Is this possible?" he demanded, slowly, impressively. "Who and what are you who have dared to insult the sacred office of the sentinel,

4

the soldier to whose lightest word even the commander-in-chief must show respect? Who and what are you?"

"We didn't mean any harm," whimpered Benny. "We're only new cadets."

"*What!*"

And here every one in the surrounding group —officer of the day, officer of the guard, corporals and privates, awed spectators—all fell back into attitudes expressive of horror and dismay.

"*What!*" exclaimed the cadet captain. "Are you mad? Mad!" he continued. "Is it credible that you, chosen by the deluded Representatives of your States to represent a proud community in an honorable profession—you dared to signalize your admission here by one of the most flagrant offences known to military law? Send at once for the Superintendent, Officer of the Guard. This is beyond my powers. Into the guard-tent with them! Batten down the walls. Station sentries at each side, Mr. Green. Put two of your most reliable men at the door, with orders to shoot them dead if they stir a muscle. Orderly, go at once for the commandant, and warn the officers that mutiny has broken out among the new cadets."

And so in another instant the luckless boys were bundled into the guard-tent, with bristling bayonets at every opening, with sentries on every side discussing in awe-inspiring tones the probable fate of the mutineers. And here might they have been held in limbo for hours had not Cadet Corporal Loring found them absent at inspection, and learned from Mr. Winn, sole representative of the quartet, that Frazier had invited Connell to take a walk, and shrewdly suspecting that they had been trapped over at camp, had reported matters to Mr. Merrick, his immediate superior, and was sent over to the rescue. Of course, on hearing the nature of their crime, he too was properly shocked, and could find no words to express his consternation. All the same, he got them out of the guard-tent and over to barracks before the army officer on duty as commandant of new cadets happened in, and had barely time to get them to their room before that gentleman came to inquire if their charges were all safe for the night. Pops found Connell grievously alarmed, but Frazier was only loudly indignant.

"All I'm afraid of is that now I won't get in the first squad to have muskets," he said. "We were going to have 'em in the morning."

But when morning came it was Geordie, not Frazier, who was put in the first squad, and Benny couldn't understand it. He who had been the best soldier of the high-school cadets was left behind.

CHAPTER IV

Drill, drill, drill! Up with the dawn, rain or shine; hurrying through their soldier toilets; rushing down the iron stairways and springing into rigid attention in the forming ranks; sharply answering to the rapidly called roll; scattering to their rooms to "spruce up" for inspection; sure of reprimand if anything went amiss, sure of silence only if all were well. Sweeping and dusting; folding, arranging, and rearranging each item of their few belongings; stumbling over one another's heels at first, yet with each succeeding day marching to meals with less constraint and greater appetite; spending long hours of toil and brief minutes of respite; twisting, turning, wrenching, extending, developing every muscle, most of them hitherto unsuspected and unknown; bending double, springing erect, roosting on tiptoe, swaying forward, backward, sideways, every ways; aching in every bone and joint, sore in every limb, yet expected to stick to it through thick and thin, until as days wore on and pains wore off, and all that was sore, stiff, and awkward grew little by little to be supple,

easy, and alert. Wondrous indeed is the trans-
formation wrought in two weeks of such drill
under such drill-masters. The 1st of July arrived; George Graham and his fivescore plebe
comrades had now spent a fortnight under sur-
veillance and discipline strict and unrelenting
as that of the days of grim old Frederick the
Great, except that it tolerated no touch of the
corporal's cane, no act of abuse. Sharp, stern,
fiercely critical were the young cadet instructors,
but after the first few days of soreness the native elasticity returned to both body and soul,
the boys began to take heart again, and a spirit
of rivalry to develop between the drill squads.

To Geordie the hours of soreness of spirit had
been few as those of physical suffering. His
years of life among the soldiers had prepared
him for much that he had to encounter, and
pride and pluck sustained him when wearied by
the drills or annoyed by the sharp language of
his instructors. But with poor Benny Frazier all
was different. A pet at home, and the brightest
scholar of the high-school of his native city; moreover, the boy officer of the high-school battalion,
of whom it was confidently predicted that "He
would need no drilling at all at West Point";
"He'd show those cadet fellows a thing or two
they never dreamed of"—it was gall and worm-
wood to his soul to find himself the object of no

more consideration at the Point than the green-
est "country jake" from Indiana or Dakota; and
to Benny's metropolitan mind anything from
either Western commonwealth could be nothing
but green. What made matters worse for Frazier was the fact that his father and mother had
accompanied him to the Point on his arrival, and
with pardonable pride, but mistaken zeal, had
sought to impress upon the minds of such officers, cadets, and relatives of other plebes as they
chanced to meet the story of Benny's manifold
excellences as soldier and scholar—oft-told tales
of how General This or Professor That had declared him the most accomplished young captain they had ever seen. Then poor Mrs. Frazier, who had pictured for her beloved boy a
reception at the hands of the authorities in
which gratification, cordiality, and respect should
be intermingled, was simply aghast to find that
he must take his stand with his fellows at the
bottom of the ladder. Luckily for Benny, his
parents' stay was limited to three days. Un-
luckily for Benny, they remained long enough to
see him at his first squad drill, side by side with
two unmistakably awkward boys, and faring but
little better. Such was her grief and indignation that the good lady declared to acquaint-
ances at the hotel that her boy should be drilling
that horrid little martinet instead of being drilled

by him—and such speeches are sure of repetition.
Before Benny was a week older he was known
throughout the battalion as "the plebe who had
come to drill the corps of cadets," and nothing
could have started him worse. One can only
conjecture what the fond but unwise mother
would have said could she have seen, a fortnight
later, that boys who had never drilled at all—
had never handled a musket—were grouped in the
first squad, and making rapid and soldierly progress, while Benny was still fretting and fuming
in the lower one. Yet what was so inexplicable
and inexcusable in her eyes was perfectly plain
and simple to those acquainted with the facts.

All over the Union now are military schools
and National Guard organizations in which the
drill regulations of the regular army are well
taught and understood ; but, on the other hand,
there are many schools and communities in
which the strictly business system of instruction
insisted upon among all progressive soldiers has
been neglected in favor of something showy,
catchy, pretty to look at, and utterly useless and
unserviceable except for spectacular purposes ;
and as ill-luck would have it, Benny had been
taught all manner of "fancy drill" movements
utterly at variance with those he was now to
learn ; and so, poor boy, the nerves and muscles
long schooled in one way of doing things were

perpetually tripping him in his efforts to master another — he had to unlearn so much before he could learn even a little. The green boys, on whom he looked with such pity at the start, knowing no wrong methods, were speedily far ahead of him in acquiring the right.

And so the boy who had entered with the highest hopes and expectations was now low on the soldier list and lowest in his mind. But for his father's hard common-sense, Benny Frazier would have been only too glad to resign and get out of it all and go home, as other disappointed boys have done, and declare West Point a hotbed of narrow prejudice, of outrageous partiality, and unbridled injustice; and Benny's mother would have honestly believed every word of it. Connell, too, was ready to sympathize with Frazier, and confidentially to agree with him that Pops, the youngest of the four room-mates, owed his rise to the first squad entirely to the fact that his father was an officer; but when four more boys were added to the first squad, and Connell was one of them, he changed his views, and decided that only merit governed those matters, after all. He began to pluck up heart, too, for he and Graham were among the first to be marched over to the commissary's to try on the new gray fatigue uniforms, and Mr. Loring's squad all appeared in shell jackets and trousers before Winn and Frazier had cast off their civilian garb.

By July 1st, however, all were in fatigue dress, and consolidated in half a dozen squads for drill purposes. By this time, too, they could march to and from the mess-hall in stiff but soldierly fashion; and still, hour after hour, the relentless drills went on. Only on Saturday afternoons and on the long, beautiful, peaceful Sundays was there really time and opportunity for rest; and still the new cadets were kept carefully secluded from the old, seeing little or nothing of the battalion, except as, with its quick elastic step and its glistening white uniform, with the brave young faces looking browner every day under their snowy helmets, with drums and fifes playing their lively quicksteps, the little column came marching down the shaded road, and the plebes were drawn up in solid ranks until their future comrades should pass by, and, springing up the mess-hall steps, give room for them to follow.

Pops wrote his first long letter home the second Sunday after passing the entrance examination, and this is something of what he said:

"We have lived together now just fourteen days, Frazier and Connell, Winn and I, and are getting along pretty well. Of course we may be scattered as soon as we get in camp, for Winn is tall, and will be put in A or D company. Connell wants to live with his statesman, Mr. Foster, in B. If Frazier and I get into the same company we will tent together, most likely. He asked me to, and said he could fix it. We got our fatigue uniforms Thursday, Connell and I, and were almost the first, too, because of being in Mr. Loring's squad for drill. He is very sharp and severe, and some of our class don't like him a bit; but thus far we get along all right. I'm so pleased to be in the first squad to get rifles I don't mind his manner. Of course it helped a good deal knowing the manual of arms, but they're a heap stricter here. [Pops would drop into frontierisms at times.] If a thumb or finger is a bit out of place, the corporal makes more row about it than Sergeant Feeny would over a recruit's coming out for guard with a dirty kit.

"I guess Frazier wishes he hadn't been so fresh [more slang, Pops] at first. He was captain in the high-school cadets and head of his class, and rather held over our boys about the drill at first; said he knew it all, and showed his school medals for best-drilled soldier, etc.; but Mr. Loring gave him fits, and put him under Mr. Flint, who drilled me the first few days, and is as ugly and stern as he can be. Frazier tried to make us believe the cadets were drilling him wrong; but when he showed us how they did it where he came from I knew it was he who was wrong; and he's had a lot of trouble, and wanted to resign and quit, but his father wouldn't let him. He's getting on a little better now, and says he'll be all right as soon as we are at our studies in the fall. I guess he will, for he's been clear through algebra and geometry and trigonometry, has been in France two years, and speaks French perfectly, and we all think he's sure to be head of the class, if he doesn't get disgusted; but he does that pretty easy. Connell is slower, but has been well taught in the public schools. Winn is a big, tall fellow from 'Kentuck,' as he calls it—good-natured and jolly. He's been to college, and is nearly twenty; so is Connell; and Frazier is eighteen, but a regular boy. He was awfully disgusted at a trick the old cadets played on him last week; and they got hold of some story about his thinking he ought to be drilling them instead of their drilling him, and I expect he'll have a tough lesson when we go into camp, where they can get at us and have fun. Don't expect any long letters like this, mother dear, when once we are there, for there won't be any undisturbed hours, as there are here in barracks this lovely Sunday afternoon. I've been thinking of all you said to-day, and tried to fix my thoughts on the service and the sermon in church; but they would go with my eyes along the row of cadet officers, who always sit in the centre aisle and at the end of the pews, and I found myself wondering what each one was like, and whether the time would really ever come when I, too, would wear the handsome chevrons and sash. I could see just where Mr. McCrea must have sat when he was cadet captain of Company C. It must have seemed such a 'come down' to go out into the world and be nothing but a Second Lieutenant, whom anybody could rank out of quarters and everybody order around. And yet that's what I hope to do after four years —four long, long years of hard work; and there isn't a happier, hopefuler boy in creation than this particular plebe. But you just ought to see how blue most of them are!

"You asked me not to use tobacco, and I won't. It is forbidden in the corps, but lots of them do it. Frazier has a hard time. He has been smoking cigarettes two years, he says, though his mother doesn't know it, and he had a lot in his trunk when he came, but had to turn them all over to the old cadets. Winn chews. He says they all did at his home. But Mr. Merrick made him surrender his tobacco—all he had; but it's easy enough to get more at the Falls. Frazier says all you've got to do is to pay some servant or drummer-boy. He has money in plenty, for his mother supplied him. They are rich, I believe, and Frazier says his father deposited two hundred dollars with the treasurer to start with, instead of the one hundred required. Some boys haven't that, and couldn't get it. Connell said he worked after hours for six months to raise enough to bring him here, and had fifty dollars to hand the treasurer. It hurts, me to think how you and father must have pinched and denied yourselves to raise the money to send me all the way, and to pay all these expenses and the one hundred dollars deposit. I know now why father couldn't afford the new uniform he so much needed this year, and I don't know what you must have given up; but I love you, and don't mean to let myself think how I envy Buddie this minute, that he is there where he can hear your voice and see your face and touch and kiss you."

But here Pops's eyes began to fill, and the letter had to be put aside. He was glad of the loud, ringing summons on the ground-floor, "New cadets, turn out promptly!" and just dashing his hand across his eyes, went bounding down the stairs to take his station in the ranks.

And then came the momentous day of their move into camp. All were now in complete fatigue uniform, many thoroughly drilled, all passably so, and all eager to get into the battalion, and figure, in their own eyes at least, as old cadets. Right after reveille roll-call on the morning of the 2d of July they were bidden to stow the last of their civilian clothing in their trunks, carry the trunks to the store-rooms, roll their bedding into convenient bundles, and be ready to move the moment breakfast was over. By half-past six the cavalry plain, as the turfless eastern half of the broad open plateau is termed, was covered with a long straggling procession of plebes, bearing their burdens over to the lively and excited camp. They had been sized the night before, the taller half of the class being assigned, as was then the custom, to the flank companies of the battalion, while Pops and Connell were told off into Company B, the right centre or color company. Frazier, always luckless, as he said, was one of the plebes assigned to C Company, and for a time it looked as though Pops were to lose his prospective tent-mate. But Mr. Merrick, in brief official tones, announced that exchanges would be permitted except from flank to centre companies, and Frazier presently found a meek little fellow named Willis who said it made no difference to him which company he went to, so he crossed over and took Frazier's place in the C squad, and thus it happened that when they trudged across the sentry post at Number Six, and were directed to deposit their bundles in Company B's bustling street, Pops and Frazier were once more together. Already Geordie was beginning to doubt the wisdom of the arrangement, but he had given his promise to tent with Benny, and would keep it. All along among the tents the yearlings could be seen indulging in pantomime, expressive of the liveliest delight at these accessions to the ranks. Pops could see them pointing out Frazier, and hear exclamations: "There's the plebe that ought to be drilling the corps," "Major-General Frazier," etc., and low laughter and chuckles. But all this was done covertly; for Lieutenant Allen, the army officer commanding the company, was standing close at hand with Cadet Captain Leonard, supervising the assignment of tents. Mr. Merrick had handed the cadet captain a list of names of those assigned to his company, twenty-eight in all, and that young soldier was now keenly looking over his new men. Pops, saying nothing to anybody, was standing quietly by his bundle of bedding waiting for orders; but Frazier, who had more "cheek," as Connell expressed it, and less discretion, did not hesitate to step up to Lieutenant Allen, and say, "Mr. Graham and I would like to tent together, sir."

The officer turned. "Which is Mr. Graham?" he asked. "Call him here."

And so in another moment Pops found him-

self standing attention to his company commander and instructor.

"I am told you wish to tent with Mr. Frazier.
Is that the case?"

Geordie colored. The question was so pat
and what soldiers call point - blank. He could
not truthfully say that he really wished to share
Frazier's fortunes as a tent-mate. In the pursu-
ance of the policy he had mapped out for himself he would rather have lived with some one
less likely to be the recipient of much attention
from the old cadets — some one less apt to be
perpetually saying or doing something to invite
their especial efforts. Mr. Allen saw his hesi-
tancy, and spoke kindly.

"If you think of any one else you would
rather tent with, I presume that it can be arranged."

" No, sir," answered Geordie, finding voice at
last. "I had thought of no one else. I promised
Mr. Frazier."

"Very well, sir. Mr. Leonard, put this young
gentleman and Mr. Frazier in the same tent—
two more with them. Have you any choice,
Mr. Graham?"

"No, sir."

And then again appeared Frazier, eager to
speak. "Connell and Foster, sir, would like to
tent with us."

The cadet officer looked interrogatively at his superior. Mr. Allen briefly nodded.

"Take that one, then," said Mr. Leonard, shortly, indicating a vacant tent on the south side of the company street, at about the middle of the row.

"Come on, boys," said Frazier, eagerly, assuming the leadership of his squad as though by vested right, and then was brought up standing by the voice of his young captain.

"Mr. Frazier," said he, "the first lesson you have to learn is that very new cadets should only be seen, not heard; and when you are heard, sir, don't again allude to members of the corps of cadets of the United States Army as *boys*. You are here to be men, if it's in you. If it isn't, you're apt to get out of it, sir."

And with this withering welcome to his company, poor Frazier was permitted to go.

"That's another young snob, that fellow Leonard!" he confided to his comrades, in low tone, as they were depositing their few goods and chattels in their eight-by-ten domain. "I'll pay him off for that yet, see if I don't." Whereat Pops and Connell exchanged glances and grins.

It took little time to arrange their canvas home in the prescribed military order. Pops was a veteran campaigner, and had slept in many a tent or bivouac in the Far West, so the quarters

that struck his comrades as crowded were almost palatial to him. When they placed their
loads in front of it at six forty-five, all they ,saw
was a trimly-pitched wall-tent, the walls themselves neatly looped up so as to allow the air
to circulate freely, the tent and its "overcoat,"
or fly, both stretched taut and smooth, without
crease or wrinkle, a square, smooth, six-inch-high
platform or floor covering the ground from front
tent pole almost to the one in rear. An elongated
wooden box painted dark green, divided into
four compartments, with lids opening at the top,
extended almost from front to rear of the platform on the west side of the tent. This was to
be their chest of drawers. A wooden rod hung
about eighteen inches under the ridge-pole ; this
was to be their wardrobe, and of other furniture
there was none. Under the brief instruction of
a cadet corporal they began with the rudiments
of their military house-keeping. First, their four
big double blankets were folded in a square very
nearly four feet across, and with the folded edges
to the front and inside, accurately piled one upon
the other. Then the four pillows in their white
cases were evenly laid upon the blankets. Then
the four comforters or quilts, folded like the
blankets, were evenly laid on top, edges vertical,
and that was the way in which the beds were
made up every morning after reveille. The pile

"'TAKE THAT ONE, THEN,' SAID MR. LEONARD"

thus formed occupied the corner of the floor opposite the locker or chest of drawers at the back of the tent. The locker was the name given the dark green chest, and the "locker" had neither lock nor key. Under the supervision of the cadet corporal the plebe quartet contributed the items necessary to their summer house-keeping. A looking-glass, sixteen by twelve, in a plain wooden frame, was hung on the front tent pole, tilted a trifle forward at the top. A water-bucket was deposited at the front edge of the platform close to the locker. A washbowl, bottom outward, was leaned against the front edge of the platform close to the bucket. A soap-dish was on the platform behind the basin. Candle-stick, candles, cleaning materials, etc., were deposited in a cylindrical tin box that stood at the foot of the rear tent pole behind the base of the arm-rack.

The four rifles, barrels to the front, were stood erect, the butt of each in its wooden socket at the back of the floor, the muzzle poked through a hole in the wooden shelf fastened about four feet from the ground on the rear tent pole. The white webbing belts, supporting the cartridge-box and bayonet-scabbard, were hung on pegs projecting from the wooden shelf. Shoes, "neatly blacked and dusted at all times," were aligned at the back of the floor, toes to the front.

Such books as were allowed were piled on the floor at the back end of the locker. All woollen uniforms, overcoats, rubber coats, etc., were to be hung on the hanging-pole. All white trousers, sheets, underclothing, collars, cuffs, gloves, etc., to be stored, each man's in his own locker. Brushes, combs, shaving utensils were stuck in loops tacked on the inside of each lid. The black full-dress shakos were, when procured, to be neatly placed on the shelf of the rear pole, ornaments to the front, and forage-caps hung on the owners' pegs. There was a place, howsoever small, for everything, and everything was to be kept in its place.

By the time the first drum was beating for troop parade everything was in spick-span order. The officers had gone about their duties, and a group of yearlings, looking as though each and every one had just stepped from a bandbox, so far as his dress and equipments were concerned, quickly formed in the company ground in front of the newly occupied "plebe hotels," the very imp of mischief grinning in the sun-tanned faces of the younger and more boyish members, but one and all full of the liveliest interest in the appearance of the new-comers and their household affairs. Comment and criticism, advice and suggestions, more or less valuable, were showered on every plebe; but even while silently and good-humoredly submitting to his fire of remarks, Pops could plainly see that no tent was so surrounded as their own. It really seemed as though every Third Class man and many a senior in Company B, reinforced by strong detachments from other companies, had come to claim the acquaintance of Major-General Frazier, and furthermore that the luckless Benny, instead of maintaining good-humored reticence, and speaking only when he had to, was rapidly adding to the array of charges laid at his door by trying to be smart in reply. The sudden batter of the second drum transferred the laughing, chaffing crowd into two silent, statuesque ranks, and for the rest of that momentous hour, while doing his best to give his whole thought to drill and duty, Geordie Graham found himself thinking, " Just won't we catch it to-night!"

CHAPTER V

THE dusk of evening had fallen on the Point when the battalion broke ranks, returning from supper. A few minutes later, a hundred strong, came the column of plebes, marching by fours, looking even more than usually sombre now in their suits of gray, contrasting with the white trousers and natty bell-buttoned coatees of the corps, and feeling, doubtless, more than usually solemn in anticipation of the possible experiences ahead of them. First night of plebe camp is a thing not soon to be forgotten, even in these days when pitchy darkness no longer shrouds the pranks of the yearlings, and official vigilance and protection have replaced what really seemed tacit encouragement and consent of over thirty years ago. Then it was no uncommon thing for the new cadet to be dragged out ("yanked," was the expression in vogue) and slid around camp on his dust-covered blanket twenty times a night, dumped into Fort Clinton ditch, tossed in a tent-fly, half smothered in the folds of his canvas home, tumbled by his tormentors about his ears, ridden on a tent pole or in a rickety wheelbarrow, smoked out by some vile, slow-burning pyrotechnic compound, robbed of rest and sleep, at the very least, after he had been alternately drilled and worked all the livelong day. Verily, the hardening process of the early sixties was a thing that might well be frowned down upon and stamped out, but it took stringent measures to effect it. In great measure the deviling system was, so far as its most harmful features were concerned, but the ghost of its old self when Ralph McCrea entered the Academy just after the Centennial year. Then little by little means were taken to make the process still more difficult to the perpetrators, until twenty years after the War of the Rebellion hazing became indeed hazardous. Officers were kept on duty and on the alert in camp at all hours. Gas-lamps were placed along the sentry post. In every way the authorities could foresee the plebe was protected from the more active torment of the old days. But so long as boys will be boys some modification must exist; and as for the year of probation which the new-comer must pass — the year in which he is taught in every conceivable way that he is a creature far apart from the rest of the corps, a being to be drilled, trained, disciplined, badgered, even at times bullied — it is really a year of most valuable experiences, perhaps the most valuable of the four. It is this that teaches him that no matter what may be the wealth or social standing of his relatives, he is no better than the humblest clodhopper of his class. It is this year that teaches him to look to his own classmates and no others for comrades and chums. It is this that teaches him silence, patience, and fortitude. Nine out of ten of the plebes and their relatives pronounce it inhuman and barbarous so long as it applies to them or theirs. Ninety-nine out of a hundred, however, uphold it so soon as their plebehood is done.

All this George Graham fully understood, and was ready to bear his part in without a murmur. Not so his friend Benny. That young gentleman had been too long the prize boy at school and the spoiled boy at home to "come down gracefully." Nothing could convince him that the cadet officers had not shown outrageous partiality to Graham and abominable malice towards himself in the matter of advancement in the school of the soldier. It was worse still when Connell stepped up into the first squad. But now, argued Frazier, we're all starting fresh again. We're all on a level to-day as B Company plebes, but the moment we are completely uniformed and relieved from squad drill under such brutes as Loring and Flint, and with our own company officers, I'll soon show them I know a trick or two far beyond them. But the golden gift of silence was something beyond Benny Frazier, and he couldn't keep his hopeful predictions or his boyish boasts to himself. He had attracted at the outset the attention of the whole class of yearlings, and, just as Graham expected, their house-warming was all too well attended.

Two minutes after their return from supper this particular "plebe hotel" was surrounded. The yearlings in force had come to call on Major-General Frazier. No noise was made. Nothing, on their part, at least, occurred to attract the attention of the army officers in charge or the cadet officers of the guard. Indeed, the latter are most apt to be particularly deaf at such times. The darkness gathered no more quickly, no more noiselessly, than did the crowd. And doffing their natty forage-caps, bowing with exaggerated politeness, cadets Cramer, Cresswell, Daggett, Driggs, Elton, etc.—one might go alphabetically through the list of the Third Class and hardly miss a name—begged the honor of an interview.

Benny, standing well back within the tent, his hand on his heart, bowed, smiled, and protested that nothing would give him greater delight than to meet the entire class ; expressed his sense of the high honor paid him, regretted that his quarters were so contracted that he could not invite them in, and was thereupon invited out, but begged to be excused. Connell was lighting the candle, and Graham, seated on the locker, was whimsically wondering what form the mischief would take, when the broom came up from behind the locker in most mysterious fashion. Match and candle both went out, and an instant later so did Benny, projected by some mysterious force from behind.

Pops and Connell were conscious of the sudden arrival from under the tent wall of three or four shadowy forms, and of smothered laughter as Benny shot forward into the company street, to be instantly ingulfed in a swarm of active young fellows in gray and white, through whom it was impossible to break away. In an instant he was standing attention, heels clamped together, knees straight, and with anything but stiffness, for they were trembling violently, shoulders and elbows forced back, little fingers on the seam of the trousers, head high, and eyes straight to the front—the attitude of the soldier in the presence of his superior officers as interpreted by his natural enemies, the old cadets. And then began the mad confusion of question, comment, and criticism; dozens talking eagerly at once, and all demanding reply, still making very little noise. The suppressed tones could hardly be heard beyond the company streets.

Benny's personal history from babyhood to date of admission at the Point was matter of the liveliest interest. No detail escaped inquiry. His military experiences as captain of the high-school cadets was a theme on which it was no longer possible for him to remain silent. With the recollection of his capture and incarceration in the guard-tent, and Graham's friendly counsel to say nothing more than he had to, and that in the simplest way, Frazier's propensity for putting his foot in it followed him even here.

In the innocence of their parental hearts, Benny's father and mother had brought to the Point certain newspaper clippings that had given them huge delight at the date of their appearance and of Benny's appointment. For several weeks he was the envied of all the boys in Beanton, the proud possessor of a cadetship, the future general, the present conquering hero; but if Mr. Frazier senior could have imagined what woe those clippings were destined to bring to Benny's door, he would gladly have consigned them, their compounders, and compositors, to the plains. In her maternal pride poor Mrs. Frazier had given copies to the mothers of other cadets less favored of Providence, little dreaming to what base uses they would come. One of these, a florid description of the review and drill of the high-school cadets on the 10th of May, and the presentation of medals to the most distinguished of the cadet officers, concluded with a glowing tribute to the "Wonderful soldierly ability of Captain Benjamin Franklin Frazier, the only son of the Honorable T. J. Frazier, of this city, who was pronounced by the judges and many veterans present the most remarkable drill-master and battalion commander they had ever seen. His promptness, presence of mind, and fine military bearing, as well as his accurate knowledge of the tactics, were all astonishing in one so young.

"The writer, who has frequently visited West Point, is free to say that cadets of that famous school are not to be compared with the high-school cadets in the precision and beauty of their drill, and *The Examiner* confidently predicts a brilliant career for the appointee from the Sixth Congressional District, who will doubtless step at once on donning the West Point uniform into the command of one of the cadet companies of the national school."

The group of yearlings had constituted itself an examining board, and was propounding most intricate and surprising problems to test Benny's knowledge of military tactics. Suddenly a tall fellow came elbowing his way through the throng.

"Mr. Frazier," said he, in tones at which every other voice was stilled, " you represent the Sixth

Congressional District of the Pilgrim State, I understand."

"I do, sir," answered Benny, eyes still to the front, and wondering what was coming next.

"Were you a member of the cadet corps of the Beanton High-school?"

"I was, sir."

"Then it can be no one but yourself to whom this article refers. Gentlemen, fall back! Hold a candle here, somebody. Mr. Frazier, we will now permit you to give an exhibition of your ability to read aloud in the open air so as to be distinctly understood by your troops. Your services as adjutant-general may be needed at any moment. Read this carefully, now." And on a foot square of card-board poor Benny saw before his startled eyes the very paragraph of all others Graham had warned him against letting any old cadet get hold of. It was pasted on the board. He could not tear it. Oh, what would he not have given to burn every word and line! "Read, sir," ordered the cadet in authority, evidently a First Class man.

"Read, sir," in solemn unison chorussed some fifty yearlings. In vain he protested, in vain he begged off. The audience was inexorable.

In low tone at first, but elevating his voice in response to imperative "Louder!" from every side, he tried to slur and scurry through, but "Slower, sir." "Enunciate carefully, sir," were the next orders, and he had to obey. Now the only interruption was a faint groan of dismay from some apparently scandalized cadet. At last he finished, and dropped the board and his eyes both in confusion. Dead silence for a moment. Then the circle widened. The cadets, as though awe-stricken, fell slowly back: The solemn voice was heard.

" And to think that this paragon has been mistaken for an ordinary plebe! It is incomprehensible! Mr. Frazier — Captain Frazier — will you have the goodness to read that just once more ?"

Frazier would have refused, but some lingering grain of sense told him the better course was now to obey. Once more he began, his progress this time being punctuated by occasional muttered exclamations — " Astonishing!" " Prodigious!" "I knew there was extraordinary power in that face the first time I set eyes on it !" " Merciful heavens! to think that we were on the point of asking a man so distinguished to sing for us !" This was too much for Connell. From the dark interior of the tent came a gurgle of suppressed laughter. Instantly two or three yearlings heard him, heaved him up on his feet, and hustled him forth into the company ground. Unparalleled audacity !—a plebe laughing at the recital of the deeds of Major-General Frazier! The circle gave way to right and left, and Connell was shouldered into the midst, and made to stand facing his luckless tent-mate until the second reading was finished. Then, even as poor Benny was hoping that Connell's coming was to distract in a measure their attention from himself, the same deep voice was heard declaring that this was too important matter to be kept from the rest of the corps. "March over to A Company!" was the word. Benny never knew how it was done. In the twinkling of an eye in silence the mass began to move, Benny and Connell borne helplessly along. Resistance was useless. Not a hand was laid upon them, but not a gap was seen through which they could escape. In another moment all B Company, except its plebe contingent, reinforced by detachments of Third Class men from all over camp, was crowded into A Company's street, and gravely presenting Major-General Frazier to the officials of the right flank company, and demanding the third reading of *The Examiner's* clipping. Poor Benny! Not until the tattoo drums began to beat far over across the Plain was he released from limbo. During that time he had been exhibited in every street in camp, had favored all four companies with extracts from his biography, and was bidden to be able to recite it *verbatim et literatim* on the morrow on pain of having to read it ten times over for every slip.

Meantime, thanks to the overwhelming interest attaching to the arrival in camp of their comrade, the general, Geordie and the bulk of the plebe class were having a comparatively easy time. They sat or stood guard over their few belongings in the darkness of their tents much of the evening until turned out for roll-call. Occasionally some old cadets would suggest that they "turn out the guard," form ranks, and render the honors of war when Major-General Frazier and his escort marched through the company street. A young gentleman with corporal's chevrons on his sleeves called Mr. Graham's attention to the fact that most of the water-buckets of the old cadets' tents needed replenishing; and Pops said nothing, but took them two at a time to the tank down by the sentry post of Number Three, filled and replaced them. This done, he was invited to Mr. Proctor's tent to see how cadet beds were made for the night, and, under Mr. Proctor's tutelage, spread the blankets, etc., on the wooden floor, and was informed that at the sounding of police-call after reveille in the morning he would receive further instruction in the correct methods of cleaning up and putting in order everything in and around the tents, on reporting in person to Mr. Proctor. In all this Mr. Proctor's manner was grave and dignified. He gave no orders, made no demands; could not be said to have exacted of a new cadet the performance of any menial or degrading task, the penalty for which, as well as for hazing, improperly molesting or interfering with or annoying new cadets, was court-martial and dismissal. Pops accepted his lesson without a word, and when tattoo sounded and the plebes were assembled for the last time that evening, forming on the general parade, as the open space between the right and left wings of camp was termed, he felt that he had got off very easily.

"Now go to your tents; make down your bedding just as you were taught in barracks; do not remove your shirts or drawers or socks; hang up your uniforms where each man can get his own in an instant; put your shoes and caps where you can get them in the dark, if need be; turn in and blow your candle out before the drum strikes 'taps,' at ten. After that, not a sound! Get to sleep as soon as you can, and be ready to form here at reveille." So spake Cadet Corporal Loring, adding, "Break ranks. March!" as required by the drill regulations of the day. And at last poor Benny, ruffled and exhausted, was allowed to go to his tent.

"Oh, I'll get square with that gang! Just wait until I'm on guard some night next week," whispered he to Pops. "You caught it nicely for laughing, Connell. Next time perhaps you

6

won't be so ready to chuckle when they're making fun of a fellow's relatives."

In his general disgust Frazier was ready to growl at anybody who had suffered less than he had. "Misery loves company" the world over. Little time was wasted getting into their blankets for the night, little more in getting to sleep. The last thing heard before the signal for "lights out" was Benny's repetition of the vague threat, "Just wait until I get on guard, then I'll show 'em."

And now followed three or four days of ceaseless drill and duty. The plebes still "herded together," as the old cadets expressed it—formed by themselves for roll-call, drill, and marching to meals. They were granted a half-holiday after the chapel exercises on the glorious Fourth, and Geordie spent the lovely afternoon with Connell and others in a climb to the top of Crow's Nest, and in the enjoyment of one of the most glorious views on the face of the earth. On the 5th their drills in the school of the soldier were reduced to two, in big consolidated squads, and the whole class began instruction at the field battery south of camp at nine each morning, and then were marched to the academic building at half-past ten, to be put through their paces at the hands of the dancing-master.

Immediately after the return of the corps from

dinner on the 5th, Cadet Corporal Loring read from the list in his hand some twenty names, Graham's among them, and followed it with the brief order to those named to fall in at two o'clock. Comparing notes, it was found that most of them were members of what had been called the first squad. No one knew what it meant until just before police-call at four o'clock, when the party came marching back to camp, each man burdened with clothing. Frazier's face was a study when Pops and Connell returned to the tent, hung their glistening new uniform coats on the rack, folded their ten pairs of white trousers in the lockers, and tried the effect of the natty dress hats in the little looking-glass. Like many another boy, Benny was learning that there was a wide difference between the official and the family estimate of his military aptitude. The idea that twenty of his class-mates could be put in full uniform and readiness for guard duty and he not one of them was something that had not occurred to him as a possibility.

"Mr. Graham, get ready to march on guard to-morrow morning," said Loring to Pops that evening just before retreat roll-call. "You, too, Mr. Connell."

And that evening the plebes of B Company congregated for an hour about the tent to see the preparations of their first representatives. In some way the word had gone around that Graham was "getting a shine on his gun" the like of which no one had seen before. Frazier, with others of his class, luckless fellows who by unguarded use of their tongues had made themselves conspicuous, were, as usual, entertaining a circle of old cadets, who demanded songs, recitations, dissertations, anything to keep them busy and miserable, and so it was tattoo before Frazier came back to the tent. Almost the last thing given to Geordie by his old friends of the cavalry before he came away from Fort Reynolds was a complete kit for cleaning and polishing arms and accoutrements. Many an hour of his boyhood had been spent watching the men at work on their arms, pouches, boxes, sling-belts, etc., and learning how to put the handsomest polish on either brown steel or black walnut. Buff board, heel ball, beeswax, linseed oil—all their stock in trade he had long since found the use of, and already his rifle and accoutrements had been touched up as new cadets never saw them; but not until this evening had he unboxed his trooper kit; and with a dozen class-mates eagerly looking on, Geordie squatted on his pile of blankets and worked away by candle-light. Ten of the plebe class had been warned for guard, and notified to appear in full uniform so that they might undergo preliminary inspection.   Nearly ninety eager boys, still in Quaker gray, swarmed about these distinguished and envied pioneers as they successively arrived. But the greatest interest centred in the B Company contingent. Graham purposely kept to his tent until the moment before the assembly sounded, but even among the yearlings there were nods of approbation and comments of "Well done, plebe," as he came forth, catching the pompon of his shako in the tent-flap as he did so, and blushing not a little in consequence. Connell, too, had patterned by his friend's experience.   Their cartridge-boxes had of course been varnished, just as were those of the rest of the corps, but the bronzed bayonet scabbards and their leather attachments wore a gloss and polish new even to the eyes of the old cadets. Luckily for the two the voice of Mr. Loring was heard ordering them to "Step out lively," and they escaped for the moment the scrutiny and question of the yearlings. But the whole plebe class heard a few minutes later Mr. Merrick's "Very well indeed, Mr. Graham," at sight of the sturdy young fellow's glistening equipments and snowy belts. Then he took the rifle which Geordie had tossed up to the "inspection arms" of the old tactics, and with evident surprise in his tone, as well as satisfaction, exclaimed:

"Where did you learn to clean a rifle like this, sir?"

"Out West among the soldiers," was the brief reply.

The commandant, with Lieutenant Allen, came along at the moment to take a look at the first representatives of the new class for guard. As luck would have it, Graham and Connell were about the last of the ten, and were at the left of the squad. All looked neat and trim, and Mr. Merrick had made his selection with care; but the expert eye rarely fails to find something about one's initial appearance in uniform that betrays the plebe. The Colonel made no comment until he reached Connell. Then he turned to Mr. Allen.

"Very neat and soldierly, especially here on the left," he said.

Cadet Merrick, without a word, held up Graham's rifle. The Colonel took it, glanced quickly along the polished weapon, and then at Geordie, standing steadily at attention, with his blue eyes straight to the front.

"You must have seen service, sir," he said, with a smile. "That's a very handsome rifle," and handed it back.

"Who is that young gentleman?" asked he of Lieutenant Allen, as they turned away.

And then—alas for all McCrea's kindly advice!

"THE COLONEL GLANCED QUICKLY ALONG THE POLISHED WEAPON"

alas for all his own precautions!—our Geordie heard Mr. Allen's reply. It was meant to be for the Colonel alone. It reached, however, the strained and attentive ears of half the plebe contingent. His days of modest retirement were at an end; his time for plague, pestilence, and torment was come.

"That's Mr. Graham, Ralph McCrea's protégé. You've heard of him before, Colonel; that's 'Corporal Pops.'"

The instant the order "Break ranks!" was given, Benny Frazier rushed upon Geordie with delight almost too eager, and loudly hailed him as Corporal Pops. The pet name of his boy days had followed him to the Point.

CHAPTER VI

It takes but little time for a boy to win a nickname in the corps of cadets, though a lifetime may not rid him of it. Physical peculiarities are turned to prompt account, and no account is taken of personal feelings. Certain fixed rules obtain as to the eldest and youngest of each class. They are respectively " Dad " and " Babe." Otherwise a young fellow becomes " Fatty " or " Skinny," " Whity " or " Cuffy," " Beauty " (if ugly), " Curly," or " Pinky," " Shanks " or " Legs," " Bones," etc., if in any way remarkable from an anatomical point of view; " Sissy," " Fanny," " Carrie," if rosy - cheeked and clear - skinned, whether otherwise effeminate or not. All these, more or less, depended upon physical charms or faults, and these are apt to be settled at the start. So, too, such titles as " Parson," " Deacon," " Squire." Others come in as lasting mementos of some unfortunate break in recitation or blunder in drill.

But no term or title is so calculated to convey with it so much of exasperation in the case of the plebe, strange as it may seem, as one which is exclusively military. Just why this should be so it is difficult to explain. The end and aim of West Point existence is the winning of a commission that opens the way to a series, perhaps, of military titles; yet let a plebe be saddled with some such appendage to his name, and all the explanations in the world cannot save him from misconception and annoyance.

From the time a new cadet is fairly in uniform and a member of the battalion, he has perhaps no higher ambition than that of being made a corporal at the end of his year of probation. It is indeed a case where "many are called but few chosen." Four out of five are doomed to disappointment, but the head of the class in scholarship stands not so high in cadet esteem as he who heads the list of officers. To be made senior corporal at the end of the first year, and, as such, acting sergeant-major, or first sergeant throughout camp, in the absence of the Second Class or furlough men, is to be the envied of almost every other yearling; but to have conferred upon one in his plebe camp by common consent the title of "Corporal" carries with it a weight of annoyance little appreciated outside of the gray battalion; and it was Geordie Graham's luck to begin his very first tour of guard duty with this luckless handle—that, too, coupled with the diminutive of "Pops."

Even as he paced up and down the shaded path of Number Three, he could hear the mischievous delight with which the old cadets pointed him out as the new corporal, and could not but hear the somewhat malicious allusions made by his own classmates, some of whom (for there is a heap of human nature in every plebe class that has to be hammered out of it in course of time) were not very sorry to see a cloud of worry gathering over the first of their number to win praise for soldierly excellence, and none were more ready — hard as it may be to say so — than his tent-mate Frazier.

Geordie swallowed it all in silence, vigilantly walking the post assigned him, paying strict attention to the instructions given him every few moments by the officers of the guard. Time and again, as a boy, he had played at walking post in front of the doctor's quarters, punctiliously saluting officers in the daytime, and sternly challenging after dark before being hustled off to bed. All this stood him in good stead now. He had studied the cool, professional way of the regulars on sentry duty, and looked far more at home on post this bright July day than any of his classmates. Both Lieutenant Allen, who was officer in charge, and Cadet Captain Leonard, who was officer of the day, said, "Very well indeed, sir!" as he repeated the long list of his instructions.

It galled him to think that when gentlemen of their standing should treat him with such respect, and when the general regulations of the army provided that all persons of whatsoever rank in the service should observe respect towards sentries, so many old cadets, lolling in the shade of their tent - flies in Company A, so many classmates skipping along inside his post on the path leading to the shoeblack's or the water - tank, should make audible comments about the " corporal on post."

His life had been spent on the frontier, where the safety of the camp depended on the vigilance of the sentry, and where no man, high or low, behaved towards a soldier on such duty except with the utmost respect. He remembered what McCrea had told him, that even as a sentry on post—indeed, more so at such times than at any other. so long as he was green and unaccustomed to the duty—it was the habit of the old cadets in the old days to "devil" and torment the plebe in every conceivable way. But Geordie argued that he was not green. He knew the main points of sentry duty as well as any cadet, though nowhere are the finer points, the more intricate tests, so taught as they are at the Military Academy.

It was actually his misfortune that he knew so much. Geordie Graham might have been spared many an hour of trouble and injustice and misrepresentation had he not been imbued with the soldier idea of the sacred character of the sentinel. It was one thing to submit to the unwritten laws and customs of the corps of cadets, so long as they were applied to him in his personal capacity. It was a very different matter, however, in his judgment, to be interfered with or molested as a member of the guard.

His first "two hours on" in the morning passed without material annoyance, for most of the corps were out of camp at drill. At dinner-time, after marching down with the guard, he found his class-mates at the B Company table, to which he had been assigned, awaiting his coming with no little eagerness; but as the yearlings began their quizzing the instant he took his seat and unfolded his napkin, Frazier and Burns were forced to be silent. Connell had remained with the relief posted at camp during the absence of the battalion, so Pops had his fire to undergo all alone. The Third Class men hailed him, of course, by his recently discovered title.

"Ah! the cavalry corporal of Camp Coyote!" exclaimed Mr. Riggs, the nearest of his tormentors. "Corporal, suppose that you found your post suddenly invaded at night, sir, by the simultaneous appearance of the general-in-chief and staff on the east, the commandant and corporal of the guard on the west, the superintendent and

ON GUARD DUTY

a brass-band on the north, Moses and the ten
commandments on the south, and the ghost of
Horace Greeley on the other side, which would
you first advance with the countersign?"

Mr. Woods, another young gentleman whose
years at the Academy had conferred upon him
the right to catechise, wished to be informed what
Corporal Graham's—er—excuse me—Corporal
Pops's—course would be in the event of a night
attack of Sioux squaws upon his post. A third
young gentleman demanded to be informed if he
had ever been regularly posted as a sentry before,
and to this question Pops truthfully answered
"No, sir," and went on eating his dinner as plac-
idly as he could, keeping up a good-natured grin
the while, and striving not to be ruffled.

But Frazier, smarting under his own worri-
ments, jealous, too, of the comments that he had
overheard from the lips of fair-minded cadets,
who could not but notice Graham's easy mastery
of sentry duty, was only waiting for a chance to
give Pops a dig on his own account. At last the
chance seemed to come, and Benny, eager to show
old cadets and new comrades both how much
more a Beanton High-school cadet knew of sentry
duty than a frontier plebe, lucklessly broke forth:

"Nice blunder you made this morning, Graham, turning your back on the officer of the
day, instead of facing him and saluting!" And

Benny looked triumphantly about him. The other plebes within hearing pricked up their ears, as
a matter of course.

"Is that so?" asked Pops. "When was it?"

"Oh, you needn't pretend you didn't see him!
I saw you; so did Green here. Didn't I, Green?
I spoke of it at the time. You looked right at
him as he came around from A Company street
past the adjutant's tent, and instead of stop-
ping and presenting arms you deliberately turned
your back on him, and stood facing Fort Clinton
while he passed along behind you."

Alas, poor Benny! Even yet he had not begun to learn how dangerous a thing was a little
learning. Graham's reply was perfectly quiet
and placid.

"I was taught this morning that when an officer passed along in rear of the post without attempting to cross it, simply to stand at a carry,
facing outwards. I never heard of its being done
any other way."

"Ho, ho!" laughed Benny. "Why, the very
first thing a soldier's taught is to look towards
the officer he salutes, and never to turn his back.
Ain't it so, Mr. Cross?" he asked, confidently and
appealingly of the corporal of the guard, who
had arisen, listening with a grin on his face while
pulling on his gloves.

"You have a heap to learn yet, young man,"

was the withering reply. " A sentry always faces outward in camp when an officer passes by, even if he passes behind his post, in which case he doesn't even salute. I gave Mr. Graham those orders myself, sir."

Pops was wise enough to hold his peace, and never admit that he knew it all before; nor did he join in the burst of laughter at Benny's expense. Frazier, indignant, discomfited, shamed again before them all, glared wrathfully at his tent-mate, as though it were all his fault.

But it would never do to let a plebe come off with such flying colors, argued Mr. Woods, of the yearlings. One after another, insistently, he pressed Geordie with all manner of points in sentry duty, and all that were not broad burlesque were answered correctly, though it was evident that Pops was getting annoyed. At last, just before the order to rise was given, the yearling leaned half-way across the table.

" Now, suppose I was to come, sir, in the dead of night to your sentry post, and demand, as your superior officer, that you give me up your gun, what would you do?"

There was strained silence among the plebes for a moment. Geordie's blue eyes, blazing a little, were looking straight into the frowning face of his tormentor.

"Do you mean without the countersign? Without being an officer of the guard?"

"Exactly, sir. Simply as your superior officer —as an old cadet to a plebe, sir."

The answer came in low tone, but without a quaver, and every man at the table heard it.

"I'd let you have it, butt foremost, between the eyes."

The sudden order for Company B to rise, in the voice of the first captain, put instant end to this exciting colloquy. Foster gave his leg a loud slap of delight. Even Benny rejoiced in the display of what he called "Graham's grit." Mr. Woods made a spring as though to come around to Graham's side of the table, but Cadet Captain Leonard, officer of the day, was standing not forty feet away, and his attention was evidently attracted. A class-mate seized Woods by the arm.

"Not here, not now, Jimmy," he cautioned. "We'll 'tend to that plebe later."

Before the guard broke ranks on its return to camp the battalion had scattered, and the yearlings of Company B were in excited consultation. A plebe had threatened to strike Woods, was the explanation, and in the unwritten code that has obtained at the Point from time immemorial that meant fight.

"Nothing can be done till he marches off guard

to-morrow, Woods," said the First Class man to whom the matter was referred. "That 'll be time enough to settle it."

But meantime Geordie was destined to undergo further experiences.

That morning at guard-mounting the junior officer of the guard inspecting the rear rank had very rigidly scrutinized every item of Graham's dress and equipment, handing back his rifle with a look of disappointment, as though he really wanted to find something he could condemn. Even a junior cadet lieutenant seems to consider it a mistake to be compelled to approve of anything a plebe can do.

But presently along came the adjutant, to whom, as was customary, those old cadets of the guard who desired to "try for colors" tossed up a second time their rifles, inviting his inspection. Trying for colors used to be quite a ceremony in itself. The color-line in camp at West Point extends along the front of what is called the body of camp and parallel with its western side. It is the line along which the battalion holds morning and evening parade, and along which all four companies stack their arms immediately after "troop." The color-bearer furls the flag, and lays it upon the centre stacks; a sentry is immediately posted, and there the colors and the stacks remain until 4 P.M., unless

it should rain. All persons going in or out of
camp must pass around the flanks of the line,
and in so doing raise the cap or helmet in salute
to the flag. It is the duty of the sentry on colors
to see that this is done. Even civilians who may
be invited into camp by officers are expected to
show the same deference.

Now an ordinary member of the guard has to
walk post eight hours during his tour of twenty-
four, two hours on and four off, but the color
sentries had only the time from about 8.45 A.M.
to 4 P.M. to cover—less than two and a half hours
apiece—and at night they were permitted to go
to their own tents and sleep, while their comrades of the guard were walking post in the dew
and darkness or storm and rain ; for never for an
instant, day or night, are the sentry posts around
cadet camp vacated, by authority at least, from
the hour of the corps' marching in late in June
until the fall of the snowy tents the 28th of August. It was a " big thing," therefore, to win one
of the colors at guard-mounting.

Twenty-one cadet privates marched on every
day, eighteen to man the ordinary posts and three
the color-line, these three being selected by the
adjutant from those whose rifle, equipment, uniform, etc., were in the handsomest condition.
Keen was the rivalry, and simply immaculate at
times the appearance of the contestants. The

adjutant would not infrequently force a dainty white handkerchief into all manner of crevices about the rifle, or corners of the cartridge-box, wherever dust or rust might collect, and a speck would ruin a fellow's chances.

On this particular morning, however, Mr. Glenn, the adjutant, was not thoroughly satisfied with his color-men. He found some fault with two of those whose rifles were tossed up, and there were only four all told. And so it happened he had made the circuit of the front rank without finding a satisfactory third man, nor had he better success on the right of the rear rank. Coming to Graham, and looking him keenly over from the tip of his pompon down to the toe of his shoes, the adjutant's soldierly face lighted up with interest.

"What is your name, sir?" he asked.

"Graham."

"Toss up your rifle."

Geordie obeyed, conscious that his knees and lips were trembling a little. Glenn took the beautifully-polished weapon, the interest on his face deepening.

"Did you clean this gun yourself, sir?"

"Yes, sir."

"If this were not your first tour of guard duty, Mr. Graham, and you had not to learn sentry duty, I would put you on colors." And all the rear rank and file closers and most of the front rank heard him say it.

Now while a plebe must be berated for every blunder he makes, and is perpetually being ordered to do better next time, the idea of his doing so well the first time as to excel the performance of even the "lowest-down yearling" is still more unforgivable in old cadet eyes. It was not until dinner-time, however, that Mr. Glenn's commendation of Corporal Pops began to be noised abroad. The adjutant, in his dissatisfaction with the yearling candidates for colors, had virtually instituted comparison between them and a plebe marching on for the very first time, and comparisons of that nature were indeed odious. And so it resulted that through no soldierly fault, but rather from too much soldierly appreciation of his duties, Geordie Graham had fallen under the ban of yearling censure, and was marked for vengeance.

This is not a pleasant thing for an old cadet—a very old cadet—to write. There were plenty of Third Class men who, had they heard the adjutant's remarks as made, and the conversation between Mr. Woods and Graham as it occurred, would have taken no exceptions; but such affairs are invariably colored in the telling, and gain in exaggeration with every repetition. There was no one to tell Geordie's side of the story. There were few yearlings who cared to question the adjutant as to the exact nature of his remarks. Without any formal action at all, but as the result of their own experience the year before and the loose discussion held in group after group, by a sort of common consent it was settled that that plebe must be "taken down." Not only must he be called upon to apologize to Mr. Woods on marching off guard on the morrow, or else give full satisfaction, cadet fashion, in fair fight with nature's own weapons, but he must be taught at once that he had too big an idea of his importance as a sentry. That might be all very well a year hence, but not now.

At the risk of court-martial and dismissal, if discovered, two members of the Third Class who had just scraped through the June examination, and by reason of profusion of demerit and paucity of brains were reasonably certain of being discharged the service by January next, "shook hands on it" with one or two cadets more daring— because they had more to lose—that they would dump Mr. Graham in Fort Clinton ditch that very night; and as Fort Clinton ditch lay right along the post of Number Three for a distance of some sixty yards, that would probably be no difficult thing to do. "Only it's got to be a surprise. That young Indian fighter will use either butt. or bayonet, or both," was the caution administered by an older head.

"Keep your eye peeled, Graham," whispered Connell to him just after supper. "Some of those yearlings are going to try and get square with you to-night."

Pops nodded, but said nothing. He had noticed that during supper neither Mr. Woods nor any of the Third Class men at the table looked at or exchanged a word with him. Frazier, all excitement, had overheard Cadet Jennings, one of the famous boxers of the corps, inquire which was "that plebe Graham," and had seen him speak in a low tone to Geordie.

"I have a message for you from Mr. Woods, Mr. Graham," was all that Jennings had said, "and will see you after you march off guard."

Pops well knew what that meant. From many a graduate, and especially from Mr. McCrea, he had heard full account of the West Point method of settling such matters. It differed very little from that described by that manliest of Christians, Mr. Thomas Hughes, in his incomparable boy-story, *Tom Brown's School-Days at Rugby*, and Pops had never a doubt as to what his course would have to be. It was one point he could not and would not discuss with his mother, and one which his father never mentioned. Pops had said just what he meant to Mr.

Woods, and he meant to stand by what he had said.

But meantime other yearlings proposed to make it lively for him on post that night, did they? Well, Geordie clinched his teeth, and set his square, sunburned jaws, and gripped his rifle firmly as the relief went tramping away down the long vista under the trees. The full moon was high in the heavens, and camp was well-nigh as light as day. A nice time they would have stealing upon him unawares, said he to himself; but his heart kept thumping hard. It was very late — long after one. Only at the guard-tents was there a lamp or candle burning. It was very still. Only the long, regular breathing of some sleepers close at hand in the tents of Company A, the distant rumble of freight trains winding through the Highlands, or the soft churning of the waters by some powerful tow-boat, south bound with its fleet of barges, broke upon the night.

Mr. Allen, officer in charge, had visited the guard just before their relief was on, and, going back to his tent, had extinguished his lamp, and presumably turned in. It was very warm, and many of the corps had raised their tent walls; so, too, had Lieutenant Webster, the army officer commanding Company A, and Pops could see the lieutenant himself lying on his camp-cot sleeping the sleep of the just. His post — Number Three — extended from the north end of the color-line, on which Numbers Two and Six were now pacing, closed in around camp for the night, down along the north side, skirting the long row of tents of Company A; then, with the black, deep ditch of Fort Clinton on the left hand, the gravelled pathway ran straight eastward under the great spreading trees, past the wall tent of the cadet first captain; beyond that the double tent of the adjutant; then near at hand was the water-tank; and farther east, close to the path, the three tents of the bootblacks and varnishers.

The four big double tents occupied by the four army officers commanding cadet companies were aligned opposite their company streets, and some twenty yards away from them. The big "marquee" of the commandant stood still farther back, close to the shaded post of Number Four—and all so white and still and ghostly. The corporal of the relief came round in ten minutes to test the sentries' knowledge of the night orders. Pops challenged sharply: "Who comes there?" and went through his military catechism with no serious error. Half an hour later the clink of sword was heard, and the cadet officer of the guard made the rounds, and still there came no sign of trouble. Twice had the call of the

"'WHO COMES THERE?'"

half-hour passed around camp. "Half-past two o'clock, and a-l-l's well," went echoing away among the moonlit mountains, and still no sight or sound of coming foe.

"They won't dare, it's so bright a night," said Pops to himself. "Only an Apache could creep up on me here. They have to come from the side of camp if they come at all. They can't get out across any sentry post."

Pacing slowly eastward, his rifle on his shoulder, turning vigilantly behind him every moment or two, he had reached the tank where the overhanging shade was heaviest and the darkness thick. Opposite the shoeblack's tent he turned about and started westward again, where all at the upper end of his post lay bright and clear. He could see the white trousers and belts of Number Two glinting in the moonlight as he sauntered along the northern end of his post. Then of a sudden everything was dark, his rifle pitched forward into space; something hot, soft, stifling enveloped his head and arms, and wound round and round about him—all in the twinkling of an eye. Cry out he could not. Brawny arms embraced him in a bear-hug. Sightless, he was rushed forward, tripped up, and the next instant half slid, half rolled, into the dewy, grassy depths of Clinton ditch. Unhurt, yet raging, when at last, unrolling himself from the folds of a drum-boy's blanket, and shouting for the corporal of the guard, he clambered back to his post. Then not a trace could be seen of his assailants, not a sign of his beautiful gun.

CHAPTER VII

THERE was excitement in camp next morning. Beyond rapid-running foot-falls and certain sounds of smothered laughter among the tents, nothing had been heard by any sentry, plebe or yearling, of the assailants of Number Three, yet they must have been three or four in number. Geordie was sure of that; sure also that they must have concealed themselves in the shoe-black's tent or behind the trees at the east end of his post. Once clear of his muffling, his loud yell for the corporal of the guard had brought that young soldier down from the guard-tents full tilt. (It transpired long afterwards that he was expecting the summons.) It also brought Lieutenant Webster out of bed and into his trousers in one jump. "Deviling sentries" was something that had not been dared the previous summer, and was hardly expected now. The officer of the guard, too, thought it expedient to hurry to the scene, and those two cadet officials were upbraiding Mr. Graham for the loss of his equipment and equilibrium when Mr. Webster interposed.

Cadet Fulton, of the Third Class, was on the neighboring post, Number Four, and declared that he had seen neither cadets nor anybody else approaching Mr. Graham's post, nor had a sound of the scuffle reached him. He must have been at the south end of his post at the time (as indeed he was, as it also turned out long after), otherwise he could have seen the marauders had he so desired. Mr. Webster got his bull's-eye lantern and made an immediate inspection of camp, finding every old cadet in his appropriate place, and unusually sound asleep. Meantime it was discovered that Mr. Graham's shoulder-belt had been sliced in two, and that his cartridge-box and bayonet-scabbard were also gone. The gun and equipments, therefore, on which he had bestowed so much care and labor, and the adjutant such commendation, were partially the objects of assault. The officer of the guard sent for a lantern, and bade Geordie search along the ditch for them. So down again, ankle deep in the long dew-sodden grass, did our young plainsman go, painfully searching, but to no effect. Lieutenant Allen, officer in charge, who had in the meantime dressed and girt himself with sword-belt, came presently to the scene and ordered him up again.

"One might as well search for a needle in a hay-stack, as you probably knew when you sent him there, Mr. Bland," said he, not over-placidly. He was angry to think of such daring defiance of law and order occurring almost under his very nose. "Go to the first sergeant of Company B and tell him to credit Mr. Graham with a full tour of guard duty, and order the supernumerary to report at once at the guard-house. Mr. Jay"—this to the corporal of the guard—"you remain here in charge of this post until relieved. Now go to your tent, Mr. Graham, and get to bed. You've done very well, sir. This matter will be investigated in the morning."

But Pops was mad, as he afterwards expressed it, "clean through." "I'll go if you order me to, sir, but I'd rather borrow a gun and serve my tour out, and let them try it again." And Mr. Allen, after a moment's reflection, said: "Very well; do so if you choose."

Whereupon Geordie went to his tent, finding Benny awake and eager for particulars. Taking Foster's gun and "trimmings," as they used to call cadet equipments in the old days, he hurried back. Mr. Allen was still there.

"Did you recognize no one—did you hear no voice—see nothing by which you could identify any one?" he asked.

"No, sir; it was all done quick as a flash. I didn't hear a thing."

"Have you had any difficulty with anybody? Had you any inkling that this was to happen?"

Graham hesitated. He knew the cadet rule: "The truth and nothing but the truth." Indeed, he had never known any other. He knew also that were he to mention Mr. Woods's name in this connection, it meant court-martial, in all probability, for Woods. What he did not know was that that young gentleman was perfectly well aware of the fact, and for two reasons had had nothing whatsoever to do with the attack: one was that in the event of investigation he would be the first suspected; the other that, having taken exceptions to Mr. Graham's retort to the extent of demanding "satisfaction," he was now debarred by cadet etiquette from molesting him—except in one way.

"I'm waiting for your answer, Mr. Graham," said the lieutenant.

"Well, sir, I suppose every new cadet has difficulty with the old ones. This was nothing that I care to speak about."

"With whom had you any trouble, sir? Who threatened you in any way?"

Geordie hesitated, then respectfully but firmly said:

"I decline to say."

"You may have to say, Mr. Graham, should a court of inquiry be ordered."

But Pops knew enough of army life to understand that courts of inquiry were rare and extraordinary means of investigation. He stood respectfully before his inquisitor, but stood in silence, as, indeed, Mr. Allen rather expected he would do.

"Very well. You can post Mr. Graham again," said he, finally; "and you will be held responsible, Mr. Officer of the Guard, in the event of further annoyance to him to-night."

But. there was none. At half-past three the relief came around, and Geordie turned over his post to Connell. There was some chuckling and laughter and covert glances on the part of old cadets when they went to breakfast, and Benny Frazier was full of eager inquiry as to what had become of his rifle and equipments. But Geordie was still very sore over his discomfiture, and would say nothing at all. No sooner had the detail broken ranks, after being marched into Company B's street on the dismissal of the old guard, than the drum-boy orderly appeared and told Geordie the commandant wished to see him.

The Colonel was seated in his big tent, and the new officer of the day, Cadet Captain Vincent, of C Company, was standing attention before him.

"There must be no repetition of last night's

performance on your guard, sir," Pops heard him say, as he stood on the gravel path outside awaiting his turn, and wondering why Mr. Bend, the acting first sergeant of his company, should be there too. Any one who happened to be on the lookout at this moment could not fail to see that a number of cadets had gathered at the east end of each company street, and, though busied apparently in animated chat with one another, they were keeping at the same time a close watch on the commandant's tent. Mr. Vincent saluted, faced about, and gravely marched away, holding his plumed head very high, and looking straight before him. It wouldn't do to grin until he had passed the line of tactical tents (as the four domiciles of the company commandants were sometimes called). Yet he felt like grinning. No one man could suppress the impulse of mischief rampant in the yearling class, and Vincent knew it. And then Pops was summoned. The colonel looked him keenly over.

"You are sure you recognized none of your assailants last night?"

"Perfectly sure, sir. I had no opportunity."

"Have you heard anything as yet of your rifle and equipments?"

"No, sir; nothing at all."

"Mr. Bend," said the colonel, "issue Mr.

Graham a brand-new rifle—one that has never been used; also new equipments. His were taken because they were the best cleaned in the class. We'll save him as much trouble as possible in the future—until those are found."

And so, instead of the "veteran outfit" that would doubtless have been issued to replace those lost, Geordie found himself in possession of a handsome new cadet rifle, bayonet, cartridge-box, and bayonet-scabbard. Mr. Bend, as instructed, carefully registered the arsenal number on his note-book. The first and second classes, breaking ranks after their morning duties, came thronging back to their company street to get ready for dinner. The yearlings promptly clustered around Bend.

"The colonel tried to get him to tell," said he, in answer to eager questions, "but he wouldn't. You're safe enough, Woods, if you don't push matters any further."

"But I've got to," said Woods, in a low tone. "Jennings has seen him already, and Ross says it's got to be one thing or the other."

Mr. Ross, the authority thus quoted, was the cadet first lieutenant of Company B. There are generally certain magnates of the senior class to whom mooted questions are referred, just as in foreign services the differences among officers are examined by the regimental court of honor,

8

and it may be said of Mr. Ross right here that he never refused his services as referee, and rarely prescribed any course but battle. There were still some fifteen minutes before the dinner drums would beat; and when Mr. Jennings came over from Company A and took Woods aside, the eyes of the entire street were on them. A prospective fight is a matter of absorbing interest from highest to lowest.

"One moment, Jennings," said Bend, joining the two; "before you go any further in this matter, I want you to know that when many a plebe might have been excused for giving the whole thing dead away to the commandant this morning, Mr. Graham stood up like a man and wouldn't tell."

"Of course he wouldn't!" answered Jennings, shortly. "Mr. Graham's a gentleman. All the more reason why Woods can't swallow his language."

"Well, see here; I think Woods brought the whole thing on himself," said Bend, sturdily. "This is no personal row, and that young fellow has been taught all his life that a sentinel is entitled to respect, in the first place, and is expected to do his whole duty, in the second. I'm not 'going back on a class-mate,' as you seem to think, but I want you, and I want Woods here, to put yourselves in that plebe's place a moment, and say whether you'd have answered differently."

"We can't back out now," answered Woods, gruffly. "The whole corps knows just what he said, and it will be totally misjudged if we don't demand apology. He's got to apologize," he went on, hotly, "or else fight; and it's not your place to be interfering, Bend, and you know it."

"I wouldn't interfere if it were a simple matter of a personal row between the two; but this is a matter in which—and I say it plainly, Jennings—this young fellow is being set upon simply because he's been raised as a soldier, and knows more what's expected of a soldier than any man in his class, and—by Jupiter! since you will have it—than a good many of ours, you and Woods in particular." And now the cadet corporal's eyes were flashing. "What's more, Jennings, I believe Woods's better judgment would prompt him to see this thing as I do, but that you're forcing a fight."

By this time ears as well as eyes of half of B Company — First Class, yearlings, and plebes— were intent. Bend, indignant and full of vim, had raised his voice so that his words were plainly heard by a dozen at least. Fearful of a fracas on the spot, Cadet Lieutenant Ross sprang forward.

"Not another word, Bend! Be quiet, Jennings! You two can settle this later. I'm witness to what has been said; so are a dozen more. Go about your other affair, Jennings."

Jennings was boiling over with wrath. In cadet circles almost as much opprobrium is attached to the bully who is over-anxious to fight as to the shirk who won't fight at all—not quite so much, perhaps—but Jennings turned away.

"You'll hear from me later on this score, Bend," he growled. "I'm at Woods's service for the moment, and I decline any officious meddling on your part." With that he strode up the company street, his face hot and frowning.

Geordie was pinning a collar on his plebe jacket at the moment, and had resumed the gray dress of his class-mates in order to march with them to dinner. So had Connell. Foster and Frazier, all excitement, had been watching the scene down in front of the first sergeant's tent.

"Here comes Mr. Jennings, Graham," said Benny, excitedly, and the next instant the burly figure of the A Company corporal—Woods's friend—appeared at the tent door. It wasn't the first time he had been accused of a bullying tone in conveying such a message. A First Class man, splashing his close-cropped head and sun-browned face in front of the next tent, emerged from behind his towel, and, still dripping, came forward as Jennings began to speak.

"WOODS'S FRIEND APPEARED AT THE TENT DOOR"

"Mr. Graham, my friend Mr. Woods considers himself insulted by your language at the dinner-table yesterday, and he demands an apology."

Geordie's face was a little white, but the blue eyes didn't flinch a particle.

"I've none to make," was the brief answer.

"Then I suppose you will refer me to some friend at once. You know the consequences, I presume," said Jennings, magnificently.

"Just as soon as I can find some one," answered Geordie. "I'll look around after dinner."

"Well, you want to step out about it," was the curt reply. "There's been too much shilly-shally about this matter already."

"That's no fault of mine!" answered Pops, firing up at the instant. "Connell, you'll stand by me, won't you? Mr. Jennings, you can have all the satisfaction you want; and, what's more, just you say that if I can find out who stole my gun last night there'll be no time fooled away asking for any apologies."

"Bully!" gasped Benny, with eager delight; and Foster smote his thigh with ecstasy.

"All right, my young fighting-cock!" sneered Jennings. "We'll accommodate you—and begin to-night during supper. See that you and Mr. Connell here are ready."

"Oh, one moment, Mr. Jennings," interposed the First Class neighbor. "Mr. Graham is possibly ignorant of the fact that as a challenged party it's his right and not yours to name the time. Fair play, if you please, now; fair play."

"Oh, he'll get fair play enough," said Jennings, impatiently.

But here the clamor of fife and drum, thundering away at "The Roast Beef of Old England," put an end to the preliminaries. All through dinner nothing was talked of at the table of Company B but the coming mill between Woods and Graham, the first of the inevitable series of fisticuffs between yearling and plebe. Of course, too, by this time Graham's virtual challenge to his assailants to come out and own up was being passed from lip to lip. Of course, it was always the understood thing that if a plebe objected to his treatment and demanded satisfaction, the offender must fight. Only, by the unwritten code of the corps, there were certain things which it was held a plebe should take as a matter of course, and not look upon in the light of personal affront; and being hazed on post was one of them. Mr. Otis, their next-door neighbor, took the trouble to explain this to Pops later in the afternoon, and Geordie listened respectfully, but without being moved. He had been taught all his life just the reverse, he said. A sentry was a sentry all the world over, and whether Life-guardsman in London, soldier in the Sioux country, or plebe at the Point, it didn't make a particle of difference to him. "I may be wrong, Mr. Otis, but it's all the fault of my bringing up."

"Confound the pig-headed young sawney!" said Otis, afterwards. "He's as obstinate as a mule, and, what makes it worse, he's perfectly right; only the yearlings can't see it, and he'll have no end of fight and trouble, especially if he licks Woods to-night."

Now here was a question. Woods had all the advantage of the year's splendid gymnastic training, under as fine a master as the nation could provide. Every muscle and sinew was evenly and carefully developed. He was lithe, quick, active, skilled with foil, bayonet, and broad-sword, and fairly well taught with the gloves. He had borne himself well in the two or three "scrimmages" of his plebe year, and the Third Class were wellnigh unanimous in their prediction that he'd "make a chopping-block of that plebe." Geordie was bulkier than his foeman, a splendid specimen of lusty health, strength, and endurance; but he lacked as yet the special train-ing and systematic development of the yearling.

"Take 'em a year from now," said Mr. Ross, "and there's no question but that Woods 'll be outclassed; but to-day it makes one think of Fitz-James and Roderick Dhu."

And so the afternoon wore away, and the excitement increased. Jennings was in his glory.

"It 'll be a beauty," was the way he expressed himself. "That plebe's a plucky one. I may have to give him a lesson myself yet." And he bared his magnificent arm, and complacently regarded the bulging biceps.

"If it's two years from now when he tries it on," remarked Mr. Otis, when Jennings's remarks were repeated to him, "may I be there to see! It's my belief Mr. Jennings will get a lesson he richly deserves."

Despite every effort to keep the details secret, nine-tenths of the corps knew that the fight was to come off in Fort Clinton during supper-time, and such was the eagerness to see the affair that, despite the urgings of Mr. Ross, the referee, and Mr. Jennings, no less than thirty or forty old cadets fell out after parade, as they were then allowed to do in case they did not care to go to the mess-hall. It was a hot night, too, and so short was the time between evening-gun fire and the opening waltz that many of the corps were in the habit of "cutting supper." The thinned ranks of the battalion, therefore, conveyed no meaning to the officer in charge. Jauntily the gray and white column went striding away across the Plain, drums and fifes playing merrily. Pops never hears the jolly notes of "Kingdom Coming" now without feeling again the throbbing of his heart as he quickly doffed his gray trousers and donned a pair of white, so as to be in uniform with the older cadets, Connell doing the same. Benny and Foster, though mad with excitement, had been ordered to go to supper. The absence of so many from one table would have aroused suspicion. One or two plebes in C and D Companies determined to be on hand to see Graham through, though rare indeed are there cases of unfair play. They had borrowed old dress-coats and white trousers. Mr. Ross had duly seen to it that at a certain moment the sentries on Three and Four should be at the distant end of their respective posts and facing away from Fort Clinton, and as the battalion disappeared down the leafy avenue by the "Old Academic," Mr. Otis came to Graham's tent.

"Now's your time, lad, and I've only one piece of advice—clinch and throw him as quick as you can."

Two minutes later, all on a sudden, some thirty or forty nimble young fellows appeared at the northeast corner of the camp, darted across the north end of Number Four's post while that sentry was absorbed fifty yards away in a 'bus-load of ladies going back to Cranston's after parade, and in less time than it takes to write it they were over the grass-grown ramparts of the old fort, and grouped about the shaded nook near the Kosciusko monument, the scene of hundreds of storied battles. Only two styles of combat were recognized at the Point in Geordie's day— only honest fighting could be tolerated at any time, but it was the right of the challenged cadet to say whether it should be fought to a finish from the word, without time or rounds of any kind, taking no account of falls or throws — the old-fashioned " rough-and-tumble," in fact — or else by the later method of the Marquis of Queensbury rules. The slow and cumbrous system of the old London prize-ring had long since been abandoned.

Acting on Mr. Otis's advice, Connell had decided on the first-named, as giving less chance for Woods's science and more for Geordie's strength. And now, while in silence the eager spectators ranged themselves about the spot, the two young fellows threw aside coats and caps, and with bared chests and arms stepped forward into the open space among the trees, where stood Mr. Ross awaiting them. Each was attended by his second. Jennings eyed Geordie, and in a gruff, semi-professional style, ordered: " Show your foot there! No spikes allowed." Graham flushed, but held up, one after the other, the soles of his shoes to show that they were smooth.

" It seems to me that your man has no business

wearing tennis-shoes," said Connell. "Rubber soles give him an advantage on this turf. I protest!"

Ross shook his head, but suddenly another voice was heard, and a new figure joined the group. A light shot into Graham's face. He recognized Mr. Glenn, the cadet adjutant who had so commended him at guard-mounting.

"Of course it's unfair, Ross. What's more, the plebe's shoes are new and stiff, and the soles are slippery. This thing can't go on until that's settled."

Mr. Ross frowned. Time was precious, but down in his heart he knew the adjutant was right. More than that, he felt somehow that Mr. Glenn was there in the interests of fairer play than he himself considered necessary, but there was no running counter to Glenn's dictum. A yearling was despatched for Woods's uniform shoes, and it was some minutes before he got back. Then the exchange was quickly made, and a second time the foemen faced each other, the yearling's skin as white and firm as satin-wood, Geordie's face and neck brown as autumn acorns, his broad chest and shoulders pink and hard.

"Are you ready?" asked Ross. "Fall back, Mr. Jennings."

Woods instantly dropped into an easy, natural

pose, his guard well advanced, his right hand low and close to the body.

"Watch that right, Graham," muttered Connell, as he backed away; and Geordie took a similar stand—clumsier, perhaps, but well meant.

And then the simple word, "Go!"

It would have baffled an expert reporter to describe what followed. Something like a white flash shot from Woods's shoulder to start with, and then for just twenty seconds there was a confused intermingling of white and brown. All over that springy sward, up and down, over and across, bounding, dancing, darting, dodging, Woods active and wary, Graham charging and forcing the fight, despite heavy blows planted thick and fast.

"Isn't he a young mountain-lion?" muttered Glenn, below his breath.

"He'll be worse than a grizzly if he gets Woods in a hug," was the reply. "Look! he's grappled!"

Reckless of punishment as was ever stalwart Roderick, Geordie had backed his lighter foe up the slope, then

"Locked his arms the foeman round."

A moment of straining and heaving, then down, down they came upon the turf, the plainsman atop. And then went up a sudden shout of warning. The next thing Graham knew he was jerked to his feet.

"Run for your life, plebe!" was the cry, as he dimly saw the crowd scattering in every direction, and, led by Connell, rushed he knew not whither.

CHAPTER VIII

"Who whipped? How did it end?" asked a swarm of old cadets of Mr. Ross, on breaking ranks after supper.

"It didn't end," was the gloomy answer. "Allen jumped the fight and nabbed the plebe. He recognized me, too, I reckon, though the rest of us got away."

And so while the Fourth Class men made a rush to find their champion, the elders clustered about the referee for particulars. Geordie was found at his tent, looking very solemn, but quite cool and collected. He had changed back to plebe dress again, and had bathed the bumps and bruises on his brown face, Connell busily aiding him. His hand was swollen and sore from a sprain, but otherwise he was sound as ever.

"We had Woods licked," said Connell, emphatically. "Graham had him down when the rush came. Everybody seemed to know which way to go except ourselves. We ran slap into Lieutenant Allen, and he had to stop and take my name instead of gobbling the others. Yes;

we've got to go to the guard - tent, they say. There's no helping that."

This was hard news indeed. Fights are so seldom interrupted, and the system is looked upon so eminently as a matter of course, that nothing but the most outrageous luck could have led to this catastrophe; and then to think of Graham's being the victim—Graham and his second—while the real aggressors had escaped scot-free!

"Not scot-free, either," said one lucky plebe, who had seen the battle and yet escaped capture—"not scot-free, by a long chalk. Mr. Woods got one Scotch lick he won't forget in a week." Whereat some of the group took heart and laughed; and then who should appear but the adjutant, Mr. Glenn.

"How is it, plebe—any damages?"

Geordie looked up through a fast-closing eye as he buttoned his jacket. "Hit pretty often, I guess, but I didn't notice it much at the time. What troubles me is that it's got Mr. Connell into the guard-house."

"Well, that's just what I've come to see you about," said Glenn. "Don't worry a particle. No one's more sorry you were caught than Mr. Allen himself, I'll bet. You've got to go to the guard - tent, but that's only for a few days. There's no dodging regulations, of course; but there you'll be let alone, and there'll be nobody to bother you. You've won the sympathy of the whole corps, and you did well, plebe." And here the adjutant put his hand on Geordie's shoulder. "That throw was tip-top!"

And then the assembled plebes would have been only too glad to give three cheers for the adjutant; but so big a gathering of the "animals" attracted the instant attention of their natural enemies, the yearlings, who swooped down to disperse the crowd, and the patrol came from the guard-tent, and with much show of severity the corporal directed Pops and Connell to fetch their blankets and come along.

And so, solemnly, the two culprits were marched away amid the subdued remarks of sympathy on every hand—even the group of elders about Ross —and in much better frame of mind than that magnate, for the orderly came at the moment to summon Mr. Glenn to the commandant's tent. That meant the colonel wanted his adjutant; and that probably meant that those cadets whom Allen had seen and recognized as participants in the forbidden fight were now to be placed in arrest.

Captures on the spot he had made but two —Geordie, breathless, bewildered, and half blind, and his second, Connell, who stood by his friend through thick and thin. All the others had scattered the instant the warning cry of the scouts was heard; First Class men and yearlings, veterans of such occasions, darting over the parapet and across the road and down the rocky, thickly-wooded steep towards the chain-battery walk, better known as "Flirtation;" while Mr. Allen, too dignified to run in pursuit, stumbled, as ill-luck would have it, on the men he least desired to come upon, if, indeed, he desired to capture any.

But he recognized both Ross and Jennings as they darted away, and saw them prominent in the ring. This meant jeopardy for two pairs of chevrons. Ross, slipping back to camp at the first opportunity, eagerly questioned Pops and Connell, who had been escorted thither by the officer. Had Mr. Allen asked them to name the others interested? He had; but, as became cadets, they declined to give their names. Glenn and Otis, the other two First Class men on the ground, had quietly retired among the trees in rear of them on hearing the alarm, and then made their way out of the gate as the Lieutenant took his helpless prisoners down the wooden stairway at the southeast angle. They had not been seen.

As for Allen's coming, it was accidental. Strolling with a friend from the hotel around the road that skirts the edge of the heights, he heard sounds from across the grassy parapet no

9

graduate could mistake. A fight, of course! and having heard it, it was his duty to interfere. The next minute he was through the north gate and bearing down on the battle, when the outermost yearlings caught sight of his coming and gave the alarm.

Ross and Jennings did not attend the hop that night. Before they had had time to array themselves in fresh white trousers and their best uniform coats, Mr. Glenn, the adjutant, had returned from the commandant's tent and gone straight to his own. Presently he emerged, girt with sash and sword-belt, and that meant business. No use for any one to run and hide; that merely deferred matters.

"Mr. Ross, you are hereby placed in close arrest, and confined to your tent. Charge—promoting a fight. By order of Lieutenant-Colonel Hazzard," was the pithy address he delivered to his class-mate, with precisely the same amount of emotion which he might have displayed had he informed him he was detailed for guard duty on the morrow. And yet seconders or promoters of cadet fights were by regulations regarded as challengers, and, as such, subject to court-martial and dismissal. Then he went in search of Jennings, and though that worthy did for a moment contemplate the possibility of hiding somewhere, he was too slow about it. Those

"'MR. ROSS, YOU ARE HEREBY PLACED IN CLOSE ARREST'"

who heard Mr. Glenn this time declare he threw a little more emphasis into the curt order.

And so, when tattoo sounded that night, Cadet Lieutenant Ross and Cadet Corporal Jennings were grumbling at their fate in close arrest at their respective tents, for, being chevron-wearers, they were exempt from confinement with the common herd at the guard-tents, where by this time were Pops and Connell, by long odds the two most popular and important members of the plebe class.

And there for one mortal week the boys remained, having a very comfortable time of it, barring the nuisance of being turned out with the guard every time it was inspected at night. They were exempt from all the annoyance of their comrades down in the body of camp. They attended all drills, and lost neither instruction nor exercise. They had the unspeakable delight of being allowed, every warm evening, to raise their tent walls after taps, and sit and watch class-mate after class-mate taking his first lessons in sentry duty out on the posts of Two and Six.

Especially Benny, when at last it came his turn; and that self-sufficient young soldier, in just about one hour's active deviling, had perhaps the liveliest experience of a lifetime. The officers in charge — for some reason that has never yet been explained — seemed particularly deaf that night. The commandant and others were not disturbed by the racket, and Benny's instruction, coaching, and testing — above all, the testing — were left entirely to the cadet officers and non-commissioned officers of the guard, and, at odd times, to certain volunteers from the tents of Companies C and D, whose costumes were so confusing that their own comrades couldn't know them, much less could Benny.

And so the crack captain of the Beanton Battalion was kept hurrying from one end to the other of his post, challenging an array of mock generals and colonels, armed parties, patrols, grand rounds, reliefs, friends with the countersign or enemies without it, that would have been simply incredible anywhere but on a plebe's post at West Point. In less than twenty minutes poor confident Benny, who had guard duty at his tongue's end and wasn't going to be fooled with, had made every blunder a sentry could possibly make, had lost every item of arms and equipments, nerve and temper, and had been bawling for the corporal of the guard, Post Number Six, in accordance with the methods of the Beanton camp, and in defiance of the laws and customs of the regular service, all to the mischievous delight of the entire corps, until finally he could bawl no longer. He had sneered at Pops for being ducked in the ditch and over-whelmed in the darkness, yet he, occupying an open post, had been so utterly bewildered, so completely overcome, that the poor fellow would have been thankful for a ditch wherein to hide his diminished head.

They had been sent for, both Pops and Connell, and questioned at the colonel's tent as to the other participants in the interrupted fight, but respectfully declined to say anything on that score; and finally, just as it was noised about camp that the plebes were to be put in the battalion, and they were fearing their punishment might keep them back, they heard with beating hearts the order of the superintendent read in Glenn's clear and ringing tones at dress parade. Even to them, in the ranks of the guard, with a crowd of hundreds of gayly - dressed spectators interposing between them and the silent battalion, every word seemed distinct.

For "inciting, promoting, or otherwise participating in a fight, Cadet Lieutenant Ross and Cadet Corporal Jennings were hereby reduced to the ranks and confined to the body of camp east of the color-line until the 15th of August." New Cadets Connell and Graham, for taking part in the same, were ordered confined to camp for the same period. All were released from arrest and restored to duty; and Pops and Connell, shouldering their bedding, went back to their tent in Company B, and reporting to Cadet Lieutenant Merrick, in charge of the plebes, were welcomed with acclamations by their class-mates.

That night, for the last time, the new-comers marched to the mess-hall as a body. That night at tattoo, for the first time, they answered to their names with their companies. Geordie and Connell, rejoicing in having got off so easily (for their punishment practically amounted to nothing but forfeiture of the privilege of roaming over public lands on a Saturday afternoon or the mornings they marched off guard), and comforted by friendly words let drop by occasional First Class men, set themselves busily to work to put their rifles and equipments in order again. During his week in the guard-tent Pops had caused his new box and scabbard to be put in his locker, well covered by clothing. The weather had been hot and dry, so that the handsome new rifle had not suffered materially.

Two days later both Graham and Connell were on the detail again; the First Class privates had been relieved from guard duty as such, and their names placed on a roster to serve as junior officers of the guard. The twenty-one sentries were therefore taken from the Third and Fourth classes, and on this particular occasion there marched on eight yearlings and thirteen plebes. As before, Geordie had done his best to have his uniform and equipments perfect. As before, Mr. Glenn seemed dissatisfied with the condition in which he found two of the aspirants for colors among the Third Class men. Going back to the front rank, he indicated two young gentlemen with a gesture of his white-gloved hand, saying, briefly, "First colors, Murray; second colors, Wren," passed deliberately by four other yearlings, Cadet Private Jennings among them, stopped squarely in front of Pops in the centre of the rear rank, and said, "Third colors, Mr. Graham."

And our frontier boy felt the blood surging and tingling up to the tips of his ears. How his heart danced in response to the sweet melodies of Strauss, as in waltz - time the band beat off down the line. How proud and happy he was in response to the ringing order: "Pass in review! Forward, guide right!" The natty little column marched blithely away, wheeling at the angles, passing the statuesque officer of the day with perfect alignment and easy swinging step. Prompt and silent he stepped from the ranks at the order, "Colors, fall out!" knowing that every eye would be on him as he passed in front of the guard. Then came the order, "Rest!" and then, instantly, in Jennings's angry voice, "By thunder! that's the first time I ever heard of colors being given to a plebe when there were old cadets in line." And every yearling in the detail probably sympathized with him.

But it was not the adjutant with whom Mr. Jennings purposed squaring accounts for the alleged indignity, but the plebe whose sole offence was that he had obeyed orders too well.

"Keep clear of that brute Jennings all you can to-day," whispered Connell to his tent-mate. "He means mischief."

And Geordie nodded. Instinctively he felt that that burly yearling was his determined enemy, and that more trouble was coming. From Woods he had had not a word beyond the intimation sent by Mr. Curtis, a quiet, gentlemanly fellow, that as soon as the excitement had blown over he should expect Mr. Graham to meet him again and finish the fight. Referring this to their First Class mentor, Mr. Otis, they were told that it was customary, though not necessary. So Pops simply replied, "All right."

But Mr. Jennings behaved with rare diplomacy. All day long he held aloof from Graham, never so much as looking at him after the first angry outbreak. That evening, when relieved from guard and told he might return to his tent, Geordie really didn't know what to do with himself. He would much rather have

TURNING OUT OF THE GUARD

been subject to sentry duty all night. However, he carefully placed his prized rifle in the gun-rack; and that evening a lot of plebes were singing and sparring for the amusement of their elders over in D Company, so Geordie went thither to look on and laugh. When the drums came beating tattoo across the Plain he returned to his tent, which was dark and deserted. Not until after roll-call did Foster strike a light. Then Graham noticed that four or five Third Class men were standing and watching him rather closely, though keeping across the street. He stepped inside, intending to make down his bed for the night; and then, there stood Foster, candle in hand, looking blankly at the three muskets.

"Why, Graham," said he, slowly, "what's happened to your gun?"

Turning instantly, Geordie saw by the light of the candle, in place of the flawless, glistening weapon he had left there an hour earlier, a rifle coated red with rust and dirt. Amazed, he seized and drew it forth, mechanically forcing open the breech-lock and glancing in. There could be no mistake; from butt plate to front sight, barrel, bands, hammer, lock and guard, breech-block and all, it was one mass of rust. Dazed and dismayed, he looked for the number, and then all doubt was gone. It was his own old rifle, the one that had been taken away his first night on post. His beautiful new gun was gone.

One moment he stood irresolute, then sprang forth into the company street.

"Mr. Bend," he cried, in wrath and excitement, "look, sir, they've taken away my new rifle and left this, my old one, in its place!"

"Who has done it?" snapped Bend, flaring up with indignation, as he saw the abominable plight of the restored weapon. "Have you any idea? Any suspicion?"

"No, sir, I can't accuse any one. It's too mean a trick."

A dozen yearlings were gathered by this time, saying very little, however, and some of them exchanging significant glances, but Bend turned impatiently away, ordering Pops to follow.

"Oh, Leonard, look at this!" he cried, as they reached the captain's tent, and a long whistle of amazement and indignation was all the First Class man would at first venture in reply.

"That gun has been lying in damp grass ever since the night you lost it," said he, finally. "The man who took your new one knew where to find this, and was one of the party that downed you. Have you still no suspicion?"

"No, sir," said Geordie, with a gulp. "I suppose they did it out of revenge for my taking colors this morning."

"Glenn! oh, Glenn!" called Mr. Leonard from his tent door.

"Hello!" came the answer back through the darkness.

"Come here, will you? *lively* —I want you."

The drums and fifes by this time were halted on the color - line, and the last part of tattoo was sounding. Bend turned away to superintend the formation of his company, but the captain directed Graham to remain. Presently the soldierly form of the adjutant appeared.

"Look at that!" said Leonard, handing him Graham's rifle.

"Hello, where did you find it, plebe?"

"In my gun-rack, sir, just now, in place of the new one you saw at guard-mounting this morning."

"Do you mean that's gone?"

"Yes, sir."

"That'll do, then. Join your company. Leonard," said he, as Geordie turned away, "the man that did this dirty trick shall be kicked out of the corps inside of six months, if I have to drop everything else to find him."

CHAPTER IX

Events crowded thick and fast into plebe life during the next few days. In the first place both the adjutant and Cadet Captain Leonard came to Geordie's tent a little after taps the night of the discovery of the exchange of rifles. Pops and Foster were still awake, chatting in whispers about the matter. Benny, who had been full of excitement and interest at first, seemed to be overcome by drowsiness and dropped off to sleep. The boys were advised by the First Class men to say as little as possible on the subject. Leonard would report it to the commandant, as in duty bound, but ask that no official investigation be made. He had strong suspicions, he said, and if the perpetrators were not put upon their guard something might be effected. Then, next morning, when Mr. Jennings marched off guard he surprised his class-mates by denouncing the whole business as a low-lived trick. Of course the plebe ought to be " taken down," but not by any such means as that. He came over to B Company street as his class was dismissed after battery drill and talked at Bend, who paid no attention to him. He went so far as to say that he believed no Third Class man had anything to do with the business; it was the work of plebes who were jealous of the partiality shown Graham by the adjutant. *There* was the man who should be given to understand by the whole class what they thought of him and his conduct! Other yearlings chimed in with one view or another, but Bend, working away over some company papers in his tent, held his peace. Jennings, who had already an unsettled score with Bend, was galled by this cool, almost contemptuous manner, and the next thing anybody knew hot words were exchanged — hot at least on the part of Jennings, for Bend kept control of his tongue and temper—and that evening occurred one of the most famous fights Fort Clinton ever saw, and Bend, game to the last, though outmatched from the start, was finally whipped. For three days B Company was deprived of the services of their plucky senior corporal, and little Hastings had to act as first sergeant while his senior stayed in hospital until his many bruises were reduced. Bend was not the only cadet whose name appeared on the morning sick report, submitted to the commandant, with "contusions" given as the reason of his disability, and everybody in authority knew perfectly well that "contusions" meant another fight; but so long as no one was caught in the act, no punishment followed. The difference between the cadet duels and those of the French fencers or German students appears to be that, though only nature's weapons are allowed, somebody has to be hurt.

But though declared victor, as anybody could have predicted he would be, Jennings was anything but a happy man. He had lost his chevrons. He had lost much of the popularity that had attended him since the plebe camp of the previous year, when his class-mates hailed him as one of their champions. He saw that now the better men looked upon him as verging close upon bullyhood, holding that he had forced the fight between Woods and Graham and then forced another between himself and Bend, a man whom he clearly outclassed. This in itself was enough to hurt him seriously, but there were graver matters afoot. Glenn had never yet dropped the " Mister " in speaking to him, and, by the unwritten laws of the corps of cadets, that meant "keep your distance." The invariable custom of the old cadets, First Class officers and all, was to "Mister" everybody in the Fourth Class from the date of their entrance until the coming of the following June — nearly twelve long months—but then to drop the formal title, and welcome the new yearling to the comradeship of the corps. Then every yearling in good standing expected to be hailed by his surname or the jovial nickname, and in return to be accorded the proud privilege of addressing even the first captain and adjutant as friends and comrades— as "Rand" and "Glenn," as the case might be. West Point recognizes no secret societies, no oath-bound fraternities. There is one general brotherhood, initiation to which occupies fully ten weeks, probation nearly ten months, but membership is for life or good behavior. Now Glenn plainly said by his manner that he neither liked nor trusted Jennings, and Mr. Rand, the big first captain, who was at first so friendly to him, now began to hold aloof. It was anything but as a conquering hero he returned from the battle with Bend. He had expected no such display of cool, nervy, determined courage against such odds. He was sore without and within, though he had received, of course, no such heavy punishment as had sent Bend to the hospital. He sat with his silent second in his tent, applying wet sponges to his bruises and noting how few were the congratulations, how indifferent the inquiries as to his own condition. Later he was lying on his blankets revolving matters in his mind, wondering what he could do to restore his waning popularity, when he heard some plebes chatting eagerly in the B Company tent just back of his own. " Graham's got his gun again all right," was what they were saying, and before he could arrive at further particulars who should appear at the tent door but the adjutant and Cadet Captain Leonard. They bade him lie still, but they had a question or two to ask.

"You were on post on Number Three last evening, Mr. Jennings," said Glenn, "and for full an hour before tattoo, when Mr. Graham's new rifle was exchanged for an old rusty one. The new rifle was found in the weeds near the dump hollow close to your post. Did no one cross your post?"

"Not a soul that I saw," promptly answered Jennings, "and unless it was found in the south ditch of Fort Clinton, it must have been hidden nearer Number Two's day post than mine."

"We have questioned Number Two," said Glenn, briefly. "He denies all knowledge of it. He says, what's more, that nobody could have got away without his seeing him. It was Mr. Douglas, of the Fourth Class, as you know, and this was his third tour."

"Oh, I can't pretend to say no one got across my post. No one can be at all parts of that long beat at the same time. It was cloudy, too, and pitch dark. Anybody could have crossed up there at the west end while I was down by your tent. If the gun was found there, it is more than likely some one did cross. It would have gone hard with him if I'd caught him."

"Then you're sure you saw no one—had no conversation with anybody?"

"I saw no one cross. I held conversation with half a dozen—class-mates and plebes both—when I happened to be down by the tank. There were Cresswell and Drake, and Curry early in the evening; they were condoling with me about being 'broke.' Then there were plebes coming down there frequently; I had more or less chaff with them, and Major-General Frazier among them. I heard him spouting about his exploits. Where was the rifle found?" continued Jennings.

"Oh, out near the east end of the old dump hollow, hidden among the weeds and rubbish," said Leonard. "But never mind that just now. It was brought to my tent, and you are reported to have said you thought it was the work of some plebe. Why?"

"Well, lots of 'em are jealous of Mr. Graham for getting colors so easily for one thing. They think the commandant shows him partiality. They say it's because Graham's father is an army officer. That's why I think they might have put up the job among themselves."

"Yes? And how did they know where the old gun was hidden—the one that was taken from him the night he was dumped into the ditch off Number Three? You think plebes did that?"

But that was something Jennings could not answer. He stopped short, and was evidently confused.

There was indeed something queer about the case. Very little the worse for its night in the weeds, thanks to there having been no dew, for the night skies were overcast by heavy clouds, the rifle was brought in by a drum-boy orderly, who said he stumbled upon it accidentally. Glenn had cross-questioned sharply, but the boy persisted in his story. It was the same youngster whom Benny had employed to buy him cigarettes at the Falls. Pops was overjoyed to get his beautiful rifle again, and, personally, well content to drop any effort to find the perpetrator. Indeed, it seemed for a time as though nothing was being done. Bend came back to duty with discolored face, cool and steady as ever, and Jennings kept away from the B Company street, where he now had few friends. Geordie began to wonder when the yearlings would decide to summon him to Fort Clinton to settle the score still hung up between Woods and himself. It was awkward sitting at table with a man to whom he couldn't speak.

Meantime every day and hour made him more at home in his duties and in the new life. Of

"THE RIFLE WAS BROUGHT IN BY A DRUM-BOY ORDERLY"

course it wasn't pleasant to be everywhere hailed as "Corporal" Graham, and to be compelled, whether in ranks or out, wherever he moved, to stalk along with his shoulders braced back, his little fingers on the seams of his trousers and the palms of his hands turned square to the front, his elbows in consequence being spitted to his side like the wings of a trussed chicken; but this was the method resorted to with one and all the new-comers, whether naturally erect or not, to square the shoulders, flatten the back, and counteract the ridiculous carriage of so many—at least, of the Eastern city boys. Anglomania in exaggerated form was epidemic on the Atlantic seaboard just then, and to insure recognition in polite society it seemed to be necessary to cultivate a bow-legged, knee-sprung style of walk, with shoulders hunched forward, chest flat, elbows bent at right angles, and carried straight out from the side; these, with a vacuous expression of countenance being considered "good form"; and strenuous measures were resorted to at the Point to knock it out of such college-bred youngsters as sought to set the fashion in the corps.

But what appetites they had! How dreamless were their hours of sleep! How vigorous and healthful the days of martial exercise! Squad drills were all finished now. Fully uniformed and equipped, the whole plebe class was in the battalion. A "live" superintendent was watching every detail of their doings. The system of responsibility among the officers, both graduates and cadets, was such that no disturbance of any account occurred by night, no hazing of a harmful nature by day. The roar of the morning gun and the rattle and bang of the drums brought Pops from his blanket with a bound. He was always one of the first to appear in front of his tent, sousing head and chest and arms in cool water, then rubbing the hard skin red before dressing for roll-call. Benny, on the other hand, self-indulgent and procrastinating, copying after the old cadets, thought it more professional to lie abed three minutes longer, and then come flying out at the last minute, frequently to be reported late at reveille, and demerited accordingly. So, too, in many another matter. Howsoever excellent he may have appeared on parade in command of the High-school Cadets, Benny was no model on drill as a high private. His wits, too, had a way of going wool-gathering, and while young men like Geordie and Connell paid strict attention to business and rarely received reports of any kind, the "Major-General" was in perpetual hot-water, and ever ready to lay the blame on somebody else. One thing he could do to perfection—that was make explanations. He wrote a beautiful hand. He was plausible, pleading, and successful. He was as full of excuse as an Irish laundress.

"He's got more reports on the delinquency books than any one in the class," said Pops, reproachfully.

"Yes," said Connell, whimsically, "and more of 'em off."

And thereby hangs a tale.

No cadet can expect to get along without ever receiving reports. Any boy who so desires can readily obtain reports aggregating one hundred demerit in a single day; yet if he receive that many in six months, out he goes into the world again, discharged for failure in discipline. The breaches of regulation in the power of a boy to commit are simply myriad. Only by determination to conform to rules in the first place and eternal vigilance in the second can he live without demerit. Even then the faintest slip — a loose button, shoestring, drawer-string, a speck of dust, a tarnished belt-plate, an instant's mooning on drill or parade—renders him liable. To utterly avoid report one has to be all eyes, ears, and attention.

Now, while it is hardly possible to get along without ever receiving a report, it is equally impossible to be perpetually receiving them without being more or less to blame. Here was Benny's weakness. He blamed everybody but himself, and, so believing, sought to convince the commandant. Before camp was over it was said of him that he got off many a report he richly deserved—a most unfortunate reputation at West Point—for there the first lesson taught and the last insisted on was "the truth in everything, and nothing but the truth."

As read out by the adjutant each day after parade, and posted at the tent of the sergeant-major, the delinquency list of the corps was a long one. Every cadet reported for an offence from "absence from reveille" to "dusty shoes" had forty-eight hours within which to render a written explanation, something after this form:

CAMP REYNOLDS, WEST POINT, N. Y.,
August 1, 18—.

Offence.—Absent from reveille.
Explanation.—It was raining. The tent walls were battened down. I did not hear the drums until some one called me. I was in my tent all the time.

Respectfully submitted,
A. B. SMITH,
Cadet Private, Fourth Class, Company B.

A cadet reported absent from any duty had to explain and say that he was on limits at the time or else be court-martialled. Except for absences he need offer no explanation unless he so desired. If satisfactory explanation were tendered, the commandant crossed off the report; if unsatisfactory, he so indorsed the paper and sent it forward to the superintendent four days later. The cadet had still the right to appeal to the superintendent, but if no appeal were made it was posted in the big record books at headquarters, and stands there yet in black and white. It is odd to read what little blunders our biggest generals made in their cadet days. Now Geordie got few reports, and wrote fewer explanations. Benny spent half his time submitting excuses.

One evening there was a crowd of visitors at parade. The band had just begun its march down the front of the motionless gray-and-white line. The commanding officer, Lieutenant Webster, in lonely dignity, stood with folded arms facing the colors out in front of the centre, the most conspicuous figure on the field. Twenty paces behind him was the long, deep rank of visitors seated on camp-chairs, chatting and laughing in subdued tones, and watching the gray battalion on the color-line. Suddenly a little mite of a boy, who had broken away from some gossiping nurse, came toddling gravely forth upon the sacred ground, and, with all the innocence and curiosity of childhood, moved slowly yet confidently on until close to the blue-and-red-and-gold statue, and there halted with much wonderment in the baby face, and began a careful study of the strange, fascinating object before him. The spectators shook with merriment. The laughter could not be controlled, and in a moment the epidemic had reached the battalion. "The whole front rank shook and snickered," as Geordie afterwards wrote home. Mr. Webster's face grew redder than his trailing plume, and he bit savagely at his lip in his effort to control his sense of the ludicrous. But when a French *bonne* burst through the line of visitors and charged jabbering down on the little innocent, only to drive him full tilt in between the battalion and its now convulsed commander, to capture him midway, and to be pounded, pommelled, and stormed at in baby vernacular as she bore him away, "Why, I just bust my chinstrap trying to keep from laughing," said Connell, "and almost every plebe in the line was 'skinned' for highly unmilitary conduct, laughing in ranks at parade." Plebes always catch it on such occasions. Geordie had controlled himself to the extent of suppressing any sound, but Benny had gurgled and chuckled and exclaimed aloud.

And yet when the reports were read out the next evening, and the plebes were holding an impromptu indignation meeting, big Harry Winn stopped and asked Graham what explanation he was going to write.

"None at all," said Pops. "I suppose I did laugh—I couldn't help it."

But Benny Frazier, who had not only laughed aloud, but uttered some expression of boyish delight, said, "Well, you bet I don't mean to swallow any two or three demerit if an explanation will get it off." And Geordie looked at him without saying a word.

Two days later the colonel sent for Pops.

"Mr. Graham," he said, "you have offered no explanation for laughing in ranks at parade; most of those reported have done so; why didn't you?"

Geordie colored, as he always did when embarrassed. Finally he said: "The report was true, sir. I couldn't help it exactly, but—I had no excuse."

"Well, in a case like this, where something comical really appeared, I do not care to see a cadet punished, provided he comes forward and explains the matter. Your tent-mate, for instance, explains it very well, and says he couldn't help smiling a little, so I took his report off as a matter of course. It seems to me you have allowed several reports to stand against you that were removed in his case. I shall remove this one. That is all, sir." And Geordie saluted, and walked thoughtfully away.

How could Frazier truthfully say he had only smiled; or worse, how could he imply that he did nothing else, without so saying, when Graham and others well knew he both laughed and muttered audibly? Geordie began to understand why it was that Frazier seldom showed his explanations.

Yet, when Benny eagerly asked him what the colonel said, Pops knew not how to tell him what was uppermost in his mind. And he had promised to be Frazier's room-mate.

That evening Mr. Glenn, the adjutant, called him aside.

"Mr. Graham, your confinement in camp will expire next week, and I understand Mr. Jennings is saying that as soon as you are released you will have to meet either Mr. Woods or himself. I have seen Mr. Woods, and told him that you have done all that is necessary; that he was wrong in the first place. Now should Mr. Jennings make any demands, I wish you to refuse, and refer him to me."

Two days later Benny Frazier, with white, scared look in his face, said: "Pops, do you know anything about it? Jennings has just been put in arrest—conduct unbecoming a cadet and a gentleman—and they say it's about your rifle."

CHAPTER X

Yearling faces in camp were looking very solemn one hot August morning. Cadet Jennings, in arrest, had sought permission to speak to the commandant; had been granted an interview, and had come back with very little of his old confident, even swaggering, manner. He had been in close arrest six days, the object of much sympathy among certain of his class-mates, because it was given out that he was to be made an example of, all on account of suspected participation in the trick that had deprived a plebe, temporarily at least, of his new rifle; which, according to yearling views, he had no business with, anyhow. Several things happened, however, which wiser heads in the corps could not account for at all. First, Jennings had sent for and held some confidential talk with Frazier. Frazier was seen that night in conversation with a drummer-boy in rear of the orderly's tent—"Asking him to get me some cigarettes," explained Benny. Two days later the Honorable Mr. Frazier arrived at the Point, and spent a long afternoon with his son; and saw him again in the visitors' tent that evening. This time Mr. Frazier senior did not favor the officers with accounts of Benny's prowess at the high-school; he even avoided them, especially the superintendent and commandant, both of whom he referred to subsequently as men with very narrow views of life. He spent a day at the Falls below, and took a West Shore train and hurried away.

The last week of August came. The days were hot; the nights so chilly that the guard wore overcoats from the posting of the first relief after tattoo. In the distinguished quartet of occupants of plebe hotel No. 2 of Company B three at least had been marvellously benefited by their experience in camp—"Corporal" Graham, Connell, and Foster. Their clear eyes and brown skin told of the perfection of health and condition; but "Major-General" Frazier looked far from well. He was evidently troubled in mind and body, and utterly out of sorts.

Camp was to be broken on the 29th, and the tents struck, in accordance with the old fashion, at the tap of the drum. The furlough men would return at noon on the 28th. Once more the ranks would be full, and the halls and barracks echoing to the shouts of glad young voices; but meantime a solemn function was going on—a court-martial for the trial of certain members of the corps. Messrs. Ferguson and Folliott of the Third Class had been "hived" absent at inspection after taps. Lieutenant Cross, commander of Company D, who was making a bull's-eye count about 11.30 one moonlit August evening, found these two lambs of his flock astray, and directed Cadet Lieutenant Fish, officer of the day, to inspect for them every half-hour. It was 2 A.M. before they turned up—young idiots—in civil garb and false mustaches. Each had already an overwhelming array of demerit. Each had barely escaped deficiency at the June examination. Each felt confident his cadet days were numbered, and so, courting a little cheap notoriety, they determined to make a name for what used to be termed "recklessness," and "ran it" down to Cranston's Hotel in disguise. Their fate was assured—dismissal—and their trial occupied no time at all. No one recognized them while away from the Point. It was sufficient that they were absent from their tents more than half an hour.

And then Cadet Jennings was called, and, as was the custom in those days, Cadet Jennings had asked a First Class man to act as his counsel, and Cadet Ross was introduced as *amicus curiæ*. The court sat in a big vacant room in the old Academic that summer, an object of much interest to swarms of visitors impressed by the sight of a dozen officers solemnly assembled at a long table, clad in the full uniform of their rank. It was also a matter of no little wonderment to certain civil lawyers enjoying a vacation, who looked upon the slow, cumbrous proceedings with sentiments of mingled mirth and derision.

Our good Uncle Sam, when first starting his army a century ago, copied the pompous methods of the soldiers of King George as set forth in the Mutiny Act, and there had been hardly any change in all these years. Lieutenant Breeze, a lively young officer, was judge-advocate of the court, and appeared to be the only man who had a word to say in the premises. Counsel, unlike those in civil courts, rarely opened their mouths. Questions they desired to ask were reduced to writing and propounded by the judge-advocate. Answers were similarly taken down. The court had been in session only an hour over the year-lings' cases when they sent for Mr. Jennings. Presently Graham and others, returning to camp from dancing-lesson, were hailed by the officer of the guard.

" You are wanted at once at the court-room ; so is that Major-General tent-mate of yours. Get ready as quick as you can, Mr. Graham. Full dress, with side arms."

Hastening to his tent, Graham found Benny already there, and in ten minutes they were on

"'YOU ARE WANTED AT ONCE AT THE COURT-ROOM'"

their way. Benny was very white and scared, Geordie silent. Lieutenant Breeze must have been waiting for them. Graham was summoned in at once. Many a time he had seen courts-martial out on the frontier, and so went promptly to the witness seat and pulled off his right-hand glove. Breeze wasted no time in preliminaries. He knew his man.

"You swear the evidence you shall give in the case now in hearing shall be the truth, the whole truth, and nothing but the truth, so help you God," he said; and Geordie, standing erect and looking him in the eye, his own hand uplifted, answered,

"I do."

"He'd tell it anyhow," whispered a New York lawyer to a friend. "That boy couldn't lie if he tried."

While the judge-advocate was pencilling a few loose slips of paper, Geordie glanced around him. The sides of the room were well filled with spectators, ladies and gentlemen visiting the neighborhood, and curious to see a military court in session. Major Rawlins, of the Engineers, was president, while two captains and eight lieutenants made up the court. To the left of the judge-advocate, at a little table, sat Mr. Jennings with his counsel. Geordie took the chair to Breeze's right, pulled on his glove again, adjusted his bayonet-scabbard, and sat erect. The first two questions were as to his name, and whether he knew the accused. Then he was told to give, in his own words, the facts connected with the disappearance of his rifle. Few boys could have told the story more tersely.

"What was the number of the new rifle?" asked the judge-advocate, and Geordie gave it. Had he recognized, by voice or in any way, any of his assailants? Not one. Had he been able to ascertain how the rifle was taken, or by whom? He had not. Was there no one of his tent-mates left at the tent the evening the exchange was made? None that he knew of. Where was Cadet Frazier that evening? Geordie didn't know; he did not see him until bedtime. Mr. Jennings was asked if he desired to question the witness, and wisely refrained.

Certain members of the court looked as though they might elicit something; but when the judge-advocate said, in response to a whispered query, "I have all that from another witness; this one knows nothing about it," the court subsided and concluded to wait.

Even as Geordie was wondering if Mr. Breeze meant Frazier, and what Frazier could possibly know, the brief evidence he had given was read over to him, and he was told he could return to camp. The judge-advocate accompanied him to the door, and Geordie heard him say to the orderly :

"I want that drummer Doyle at once. Why is he not here?"

"We can't find him, sir, anywhere," was the answer.

"Well, go again, and tell the drum-major to have him hunted up. He had no business to let him away from barracks."

As Geordie started out into the open air, he caught sight of Benny's woe-begone face. What could have happened to him?

"Detained as a witness before the court-martial," said the officer of the day to whom Frazier was reported absent at dinner roll-call; but Pops found him lying on his bedding when they got back to camp. He didn't want to talk, he said; his head was aching. He was all upset about something, that was evident. No, he didn't want any dinner. Jennings and his counsel had joined the battalion at the mess-hall with unimpaired appetites and confident mien. The plebe it was who seemed all gone to pieces. By parade-time a strange story had come into the camp by way of the visitors' tent. Court had adjourned until the witness Doyle could be found, and Mr. Frazier, whose testimony it was supposed would materially harm the accused, had not harmed his case at all. In brief, Frazier, acting under in-

11

structions evidently, tremblingly admitted that he was aware of some joke being played on his tent-mate that night, but refused to answer questions on the ground that answers might incriminate himself. The sensation among the plebes was tremendous. Everybody jumped to one conclusion—Frazier must have taken part in "the robbery," as they now began to call it.

But Mr. Ross came to the rescue. "Wait until you hear the whole story," he said. "It can't be told now, but will be when the excitement has died away and it is safe to tell it."

And so the youngsters had to wait. Connell and Foster seemed to shrink from their classmate instinctively. It was Graham who simply would not believe that ill of him.

"I can't tell as yet. I've given my word to Ross and Jennings," said Benny, with a wail in his voice. "Don't go back on me, Graham, and you'll never regret it." And, taking the side of "the under dog in the fight," Geordie held out his hand.

The 28th came, and still no tidings of the missing witness. Doyle, the drummer, had vanished, and no one knew whither. The furlough-men came back at mid-day, looking probably for the same tumultuous greeting that had been accorded their predecessors for years back — a charge of the First and Third Classes from camp, and a smashing of Derby hats—but they were marshalled direct to barracks instead, and, completely uniformed and equipped, marched over to join the battalion in style most matter of fact. The plebes spent the last evening in camp listening to the distant music of the hop, and singing, reciting, and dancing for the benefit of the returned Second Class men. Certain celebrities of their number were, with appropriate ceremonies, presented to such Second Class men as preferred "devilment" to dancing, among them "Corporal Pops, the coyote-killer of the Colorado, famous as bear-hunter, scalp-taker, and sign-talker," and for the last time Geordie was on duty entertaining old cadets until the tattoo drums, but no one turned out Benny Frazier. A yearling will not even have fun at the expense of a plebe whose conduct is considered shady, and the belief in the Third Class was general that Frazier, through motives of jealousy, had connived at the "hiving" of his tent-mate's rifle.

And yet when Connell said to Graham, "I was going to room with Foster, but I'd far rather live with you. Do you think we can fix it now? Foster is willing to live with Clawson," he could hardly believe it when Geordie answered:

"I've promised to live with Frazier, and though I'd rather live with you than any man I know, I won't go back on my promise."

Geordie did not tell what he might have told. that on the evening of the 27th, after a long talk with his father, who came at noon and left before parade, Frazier had almost pleadingly said to him: "They're all down on me now, Graham, and if you turn from me I won't have a friend left in the class. If you and I room together, they'll know you don't believe me mean enough to take your gun. Appearances are all against me simply because I can't tell without involving some poor fellows whom dismissal would ruin for life just because they'd taken part in what they meant to be only a joke." And Graham answered that he meant to stand by Frazier until the thing was all cleared up.

There were plebes who came to Geordie and told him he was making a mistake. So did Mr. Otis, but the latter went away all the more convinced that "Corporal Pops" was too pig-headed even for a Scot. It was almost pitiful to see the way Frazier clung to his companion now. It looked to everybody as though the boy were jealously afraid of seeing his friend and protector, so called, talking with anybody else. Time and time again he reminded Pops of the agreement, until at last, annoyed, Geordie turned suddenly upon him and said:

"Look here, Frazier, does nobody keep promises where you come from?"

Then Benny concluded it was time to hold his peace.

In the presence of a thousand spectators on a glorious August day, every tent in camp went down at the tap of the drum, and what an instant before had been a white-roofed city turned into a bustling hive of gray coats, folding, rolling, and cording up the snowy canvas. All baggage had been moved to barracks earlier in the day, and now in full ranks, all four classes present, the companies fell in, and the corporals, who had served all summer long as sergeants, stepped back into the ranks, and the plebes gazed in silent awe upon the grave, dignified young soldier in the white cross-belts and crimson sash who so keenly looked them over before reporting " All present, sir," to Mr. Leonard. The returned furlough-men took their places, as became members of the Second Class, in the front rank. Certain yearlings, much to their disgust, had to fall back to the rear, and as far as faces could be seen at all any one could distinguish which was which. The boys who had spent the summer in camp were brown as autumn berries ; they who had spent their summer at home were pallid by contrast.

For the last time in camp adjutant's call sounded on the color-line, and the band had to take station beyond the sentry on Number Two, in order to leave room for the re-enforced battalion.

"Guides posts!" rang out the adjutant's command.

"Keep your eyes to the front, plebe," ordered the red-sashed first sergeant, returning to his station through the gap on the right, when he found two Fourth Class men gazing obliquely at him in mingled awe and admiration.

Clash! went the rifles into the gloved left hands as the battalion presented arms to Colonel Hazzard.

"Take your post, sir," was that eminent soldier's response to Glenn's superb salute. Back to his station on the right fluttered the adjutant's plumes as the companies wheeled into column, tossed the light rifles to the shoulder, and then, to the merriest, blithest of music, strode buoyantly away in the wake of the band, the drum-major boring with his tasselled baton a hole through the heart of the crowd.

Geordie's pulses beat high with every stride. Welcome hard work, hard study, even the long gloomy wintry weeks and months, for plebe camp and palms-of-the-hands-to-the-front were now things of the past.

That night Glenn read the list of sections to which the classes were assigned. Great was the importance of certain Fourth Class men designated in orders as section marchers, and by no means inconsiderable was the jealousy among their class-mates inspired by this purely accidental and temporary gift of authority. The Fourth Class for instruction in mathematics was divided in alphabetical order into eight sections, Cadet Abbott being detailed as marcher of the first, Dillon of the second, Griggs of the third, Kenney of the fourth, and so on down the list. Frazier, who had been very meek for several days, asked Graham if he didn't think it extraordinary that they should be ordered around by a fellow like Dillon?

"Why, I don't believe I've ever heard him speak ten words. What makes them put such galoots in command of sections when there's others, like you, for instance, that know how to handle 'em?"

Pops grinned. He understood what Benny was thinking of.

"It's all part and parcel of the system of teaching fellows like me, as you put it, that obedience is the first thing we have to learn," said he, good-naturedly, and then went busily on with the work of getting the room in the prescribed order.

As plebes they had enjoyed only what is termed "Hobson's choice." They could have either the top or bottom floor on the north front of barracks—the cold, sunless front—and so they found themselves in the third division, or, as it was technically termed, the "Third Div. Cockloft"; that meant on the top floor of the third division from the east. It took little time to arrange their household affairs. Each cadet had his own alcove or bedroom, separated one from the other by a wooden partition. On the side nearest the wall was a light iron bedstead; on this a single mattress, folded back during the day, and made down only after tattoo. Piled in order on the mattress, folded edges to the front, and vertical, were first the sheets, then pillows, then blankets and "comfortable." On iron hooks in the partition, each in his own alcove, and in the following order from front to rear, the boys hung their overcoats, rubber coats (once called the "plebeskins"), the uniform coats, gray jackets, gray trousers, "such underclothing as may be allowed," and at the rearmost end the clothes-bag for soiled clothing. Against the front post of the partition was the little wooden wash-stand, a bucket of water, with cocoa-nut dipper, on the bottom shelf the white washbowl, inverted, with soap-dish, etc., on top; a slop-bucket on the side opposite the hall; a little mirror in the middle of the mantel-shelf; rifles in the rack near window; dress hats on the shelf thereof; accoutrements and forage-caps hung on the pegs to the right and left of the rack; candle-box in the fireplace (which was neatly whitewashed); nothing on the steam

coil or heater; all other clothing in the open-faced
set of shelves termed the clothes-press; brushes,
combs, shaving materials, collars, cuffs, handker-
chiefs, belts, and gloves, each folded or stacked in
separate piles on the upper shelf; shirts, etc., on
the next below; white trousers, underclothing,
etc., on the lowermost, and nothing under it; text-
books on the top of the press against the wall,
upright, and backs to the front; broom behind the
door; chairs, when not in use, against the table;
table against the wall opposite the fireplace; shoes
aligned at the foot of the bed, toes to the front,
and always to be kept neatly dusted; "clocks,
pictures, statuettes, etc., not allowed."

Everything was kept in spick-span order, and
the orderly board, giving the name of the cadet
responsible for the general appearance of things
during the week, hung on the pillar of the alcove
partition. Each cadet posted his own name in
plain block letters over the alcove, over his half
of the clothes-press, over his equipments, etc., and
on the back of the door his " hours of recitations,"
to account for his absence from the room at any
inspection. For half an hour after breakfast, dinner, or supper, and on Saturday afternoons, cadets could visit in barracks, or go from room to
room. At any other time and during call to
quarters, day or night, visiting, even to the extent of opening and looking in one's next door

neighbor's door, was punishable by demerit and confinement.

When little Dillon came around to give out the first lesson in algebra, as received from their section instructor, Lieutenant Barnes, Pops was all attention, and carefully noted it in his new algebra. Benny wanted to chaff Mr. Dillon by asking him if he supposed he could march a squad as far as the Academic, and was suddenly reminded of his uncertain status by being curtly told to mind his own business. In ten minutes Pops was deep in his work, but Frazier, giving a sniff of contempt on glancing over the pages, tossed his text-book on the table, went to the window and, strumming on the glass, gazed long and wearily out upon the starlit sky. This being a West Point cadet wasn't what it was represented to be by a good deal.

CHAPTER XI

Mid - September came, and with it certain changes. The court-martial which had been in session during the latter part of camp stood adjourned, awaiting the call of its president. It was understood that, owing to the unaccountable disappearance of a material witness, the case of Cadet Jennings could not be pressed. Musician Doyle had totally vanished, no man could tell whither. He had left his "kit" and his few belongings at the barracks down in Camptown, and had taken with him only the clothes he had on, said the drum-major. Some people thought he was drowned, but most believed that he had deserted. He was last seen at the Falls the night before the convening of the court. In the meantime, Mr. Jennings remained in arrest with extended limits, which meant that he had the privilege of exercising in the gymnasium and walking the area, but could enter no division in barracks other than his own. The two yearlings tried at the same time with him were quietly summoned to the office of the commandant one day and told to pack their trunks. They were out of uniform and off the Point before the order of the War Department was read that evening at parade dismissing them from the service. Benny Frazier was recovering his self-confident manner, and rapidly losing the meekness of spirit displayed during his troublous days the last week in camp, and Pops was losing something of his splendid brown color, and not a few hours of sleep.

In very truth Geordie's hard times were at hand. He was not a natural mathematician, and the lessons in algebra, so carelessly conned and tossed aside by his gifted room-mate, were proving long and hard to our young trooper. Barrack life differed very materially from that of camp. Reveille came at the same hour, the gun and the drums letting drive together at the first stroke of 5; the drummers came marching in across the Plain and through the resounding sally-port, then rattled and banged a moment, one in each hallway, then reunited in the area, and by 5.10 the whole corps would be jumped into ranks at the brisk assembly, about one-fourth of their number rushing out only at the last instant. Then came the rapid roll-call, the few moments of sweeping and dusting before police inspection, the brief soldier toilet, the march to breakfast, etc. There was time for study before the first recitation for all those studiously disposed—which most of the corps had to be—and then at 7.55 the bugle summoned one-half the entire battalion to recitation—the First Class to engineering, the Second to mechanics, the Third to analytical geometry, and the Fourth to algebra; the highest sections in each reciting, as a rule, first hour, and the first hour at West Point meant just half an hour longer than it does anywhere else. The sections began recitation by 8.5, and were recalled by the bugle at 9.30, at which time the other half of the battalion was formed and marched, each section by its own marcher, to the rooms vacated by the upper half of the class.

One word now about West Point recitations. The section-rooms were severity itself in their furniture, which consisted only of blackboards or slates on three sides of each room, two long benches, one on each side, a wooden desk and chair on a little wooden dais between the windows for the instructor. There used to be a stove in the centre, in case of mishap to the steam supply, and that was all, unless chalk, pointers, and erasers were counted. In soldierly silence the section marched to the door, hung their caps on pegs outside, went to their places, stood attention, facing inwards, while the marcher reported, "All are present, sir," then took their seats. On the slate back of the instructor were written the page and paragraph to which next day's lesson extended, and it was each cadet's business to note it. No time was lost. The instructor, a lieutenant especially distinguished for scholarship while a cadet, called up his pupils one after another, giving to the first four demonstrations to work out on the front boards from the lesson of the day. The next four were sent to the side boards with problems on leading points in the lesson of the previous day, and the ninth man "jumped" to the floor and was put through a cross-examination in some subject under discussion that was intended to thoroughly sound the depth of his knowledge. Each cadet on being called stepped to the centre of the floor, "stood attention," facing the instructor, received his enunciation, faced about, went to the board, wrote his name and the order in which he was called up (that is, first, second, or third) in the upper right-hand corner, then went to work. No communication of any kind was allowed. As soon as his work was finished the cadet faced about, stood at ease until called upon to recite, then, pointer in hand, he began: "I am required to discuss the Problem of the Lights," or "I am required to deduce a rule for such and such a purpose," or, generally, whatsoever his task might be. Then he proceeded in his own words to do it.

All this time the instructor sat quietly listening and mentally criticising. The whole idea of the West Point system is that the reciting cadet becomes for the time being the instructor, endeavoring to explain the subject to somebody who knows nothing at all of the matter. Then comes the instructor's turn. If the recitation has been full, every point fairly, squarely met and covered, not a jot or tittle requiring further elucidation, the instructor generally says, " Very well, sir, that 'll do," and the young gentleman goes to his seat sure of a " max.," or " 3," on the weekly list. If the instructor has to ask a question or two in order to establish the pupil's thorough knowledge, 2.9 or 2.8 may result; 2.5 is really a good mark; 2 is fair; 1.5 what would be called " fair to middling " on 'Change; 1 is only tolerable, and zero a flat and utter failure, or its equivalent, a statement that the cadet doesn't " know enough about it to attempt a recitation." Many a cadet has taken zero and a report for neglect of studies rather than make a bungling performance, but the instructors are ordinarily men of such mould that they soon get to gauge their pupils thoroughly, and instead of letting a young fellow doom himself to failure, they patiently question, " draw him out," and there demonstrate that he knows not a little of the subject, and mark him accordingly. Recitations go on every morning in the week, Sundays alone excepted.

The West-Pointer has only one half-holiday, and that Saturday afternoon, and then only those whose conduct has been up to the mark can enjoy it—confinement to quarters, or " walking punishment tour," being the fate of many a boy regularly as the day comes round. And so by Saturday the cadet has recited five, or possibly six, times in the morning recitations, and on Monday the class reports are published, showing the exact standing in every study of every man in the corps. It is comical sometimes at the start to see how the plebes attempt to work off the time - honored excuses of the school-boy. They are worthless at the Point. Even if he were really so ill he could not study, the cadet cannot be excused by the instructor. The young gentleman has to go to his first sergeant at reveille, ask to have his name put on the sick-book; then when sick-call sounds he is marched down to the hospital and states his case to the doctor, who can order him into hospital if the matter be at all serious, or prescribe some remedy, and mark him excused from first recitation, from drill, or whatever may be necessary. Now anywhere else that would mean " excused from *attending* recitation," but not at West Point. Unless actually in hospital and under medical care the cadet must go to the recitation - room with his class, there report to the instructor, "I am excused from reciting, sir." The fact is noted on the record for the day, and, taking his seat, the cadet follows his comrades' work as best he may.

While one-half the corps is at recitation, the other half, each cadet in his own room, is required to be at study; no visiting is allowed. At 11 the heavier recitations are over for the day. From this hour on the time given to each is only about fifty-five minutes in the section-room. At 12.55 the first drum beats for dinner. All sections are then dismissed; books are hurriedly returned to rooms, and by 1.5, in solid ranks, the battalion is marching down to Grant Hall. From the time they get back to barracks — about 1.35 — until the bugle again sounds at 2, is release from quarters. At 2, recitations begin again. Law, languages, drawing, drill regulations, or something of that character, take up the afternoon until 4, then all are marched (and it is march, march all the time) to barracks, where they have five minutes in which to get ready for afternoon drill. In September the school of the battalion is the prescribed exercise, followed by parade at sunset, these giving way in October, as the days become shorter, to artillery drills at the various batteries. Supper comes after parade, and evening "call to quarters;" study hour, thirty minutes after the return of the battalion from supper. Study goes on until tattoo, which, when Pops was at the Point, was sounded at 9.30, followed by taps at 10. Each cadet was expected to make down his bedding for the night at tattoo, and to be in bed, undressed, and with his light extinguished when the drum sounded at 10 o'clock. Officers of the First Class and cadet staff and first sergeants of the Second Class were the exceptions. These were permitted lights until 11, the cadet officers being assigned to duty all over barracks as inspectors of sub-divisions, each one having two floors, or eight rooms, under his control, and these he was to inspect at morning police call and at taps.

What with turning out at 5 A.M. and studying, reciting, exercising in the gymnasium or on drill, the plebes, at least, were ready to go to bed at 9.30; some found it impossible to keep awake until then.

Such being the general programme, let us see how it applied to Geordie and Frazier. The former was fidelity itself in his desire to observe regulations and perform his duty. Benny, eager and enthusiastic at first, was rapidly developing traits that proved him to be just the reverse. Week and week about each became responsible for the condition of the room, his name being posted as orderly. They were in the subdivision

of Cadet Lieutenant Webb, the first officer to inspect their room each day. Later came the in-
spections made by the cadet officer of the day,
and, almost invariably, morning and evening, a
visit from Lieutenant Allen, the commandant
of Company B (or "the B Company tack," as
termed in the corps). If at any one of these in-
spections anything was found amiss—chairs or
broom, caps or accoutrements, washbowl or
buckets or books out of place, dust on mantel or
dirt on floor—the inspector never stopped to ask
who was at fault; he simply glanced at the orderly-board to see who was responsible, and
down went that gentleman on the delinquency
book, and that meant — unless the report were
removed—so many demerit and so much light
punishment.

Pops found no trouble in keeping himself and
his room in order, but he couldn't keep Benny.
Before the 25th of September, " Graham, orderly," had been reported four times for things he
really could not help, and all due to Benny's
careless habits. Once it was washbowl not .in-
verted, another time broom out of place, and
twice chairs out of place. Benny, the last one
to use these items during his room - mate's absence, had left them as found by the inspector.
Pops remonstrated, gently at first, but afterwards sternly, and Frazier either sulked or else

swore he left everything all right; "somebody must have come in and upset them."

This was bad enough, but worse was to follow. Before the end of the month, every Saturday evening at parade, the adjutant was busily reading "transfer orders," principally in the Fourth Class. Fluent in recitation, Benny Frazier had made a brilliant start. This part of mathematics he had been over time and again, and he was transferred to the first section at the first order. At the second order, along about the 20th, poor Geordie heard with heavy heart his own name read out for transfer, not up, but down. "Cadet Graham to the fourth section." He had worked hard, very hard. He studied faithfully every possible moment, while Benny was listlessly yawning, dozing, or scribbling. A few minutes conning over the familiar pages put him at his ease as to the lesson of the morrow, while Graham worked on with reddening eyelids. Sometimes the latter would appeal to Frazier to explain points that were perplexing to him, and Benny at first seemed rather pleased to do so, but he was no patient instructor, and not especially gifted in the method of proving why this or that was thus and so. He thought Geordie ought to see it all at a glance.

What with going up to the first section at a bound and believing himself on the high-road

"'I WANT YOU TO COME AND WALK WITH ME,' CONNELL SAID"

to the head of the class, coupled with the fact that now there was so very little time given to anything but recitation and study, Benny began to look upon himself as out of the shadow and into the sunshine of prosperity once more. Then came an order releasing Mr. Jennings from arrest. No case had been established. The court simply had to acquit him. The rifle affair was being forgotten in the press of other matters. "Nothing succeeds like success." Class-mates could not but admire Frazier's fluency in recitation, and Graham, silent, reserved, studying day and night, was not the prominent figure in his class-mates' eyes he had been in camp. Presently Benny's manner, from having been meek and appealing, began to be patronizing and superior. Then as pride and confidence reasserted themselves he began to chafe at any authority over him. The third week in barracks Frazier got four reports as room orderly; the fourth week Pops's name was hoisted to the top of the orderly-board, and he gravely told Benny he hoped he'd be careful.

That very evening after supper Connell took Geordie's arm and led him out on the Plain.

"I want you to come and walk with me, old man," he said. "You were going to your room to 'bone,' and I know it. Pops, don't do that. What time we have to spend in the open air

you need to take for no other purpose. You'll
go to your work with a clearer head."

Geordie protested, but he knew Connell was
right. Moreover, letters had come that very day
from McCrea and the doctor, both bidding him
feel no discouragement because he was making
only an average of less than 2.5, "even if you
do go down two or three sections," wrote the
lieutenant; "and I was scared badly because they
sent me from the fifth down to the sixth, but I
came out all right." The doctor, too, urged that
his boy take heart, and bade him neglect no regular out-door exercise. A great believer in fresh
air and sunshine was the doctor. Still, Pops
was blue. Connell, a Western lad, with only the
drilling of the public schools, had managed to
cling to his place in the first section, and with
every day was becoming more and more at home
in the methods of the section-room.

"Doesn't Frazier help you?" he asked.

"Not much. He's generally busy reading,
writing, or dozing, and he's impatient of my
stupidity, I suppose. Everything seems so easy
to him," answered Pops.

"Yes, I never heard such finished recitations.
'Old Scad' just sits there and nods approval, and
seldom asks a question." ("Old Scad" was the
irreverent title given to a gray-headed lieutenant of artillery by a previous class, and plebes

rarely fail to adopt such nicknames.) "Benny's 'maxing' right along just now," continued Connell.

"Do you think he'll be head of the class?" asked Pops.

Connell pondered a moment before replying. "He might, because he's just as fluent in French; but I'll bet my hopes of graduation against the corporal chevrons you're bound to wear next June that if he's head in January he'll never get there again."

"Why, Con? What do you mean?"

"Simply this: Frazier is a sort of fireworks fellow. He's going up with a flash and a roar, but he'll burn out by the time we get into analytical. He isn't a stayer. Mr. Otis was telling me last night that there were cases where fellows who stood head in the plebe January dropped out of sight by the end of the third year. As for Frazier, he'll get found on demerit if he isn't careful. He's smoking cigarettes again. Don't let him light one in the room."

"Oh, he doesn't so long as I am there. Of course if I get reported as orderly for tobacco smoke in quarters he'll be man enough to take it off my shoulders."

Connell was silent a moment, then he spoke: "I don't want to wrong Frazier, but I'm inclined to think that the less you build on his doing the manly thing at his own expense the safer you'll be."

And that evening, as Geordie returned to his room, all in a glow from the brisk walk, he found a party of plebes just breaking up and scattering to their quarters. Benny had been "entertaining," and the air was full of cigarette smoke. Vigorous fanning with the door and with towels swept much of the smoke out through the open window, but the aroma of the heavy, drug-scented cloud hovered over the occupants' heads.

"You knew what would happen. How could you be so reckless of other fellows' rights?" said Graham, angrily.

Benny flared up at once. He wasn't going to forbid gentlemen smoking when they came to see him! There was no danger, anyhow! They'd fan out the room before Allen could come, and by hard work they did. Mr. Allen looked queer, but said nothing. "Didn't I tell you!" cried Benny.

"All the same," answered Pops, "there must be no more of it when I'm orderly."

"I'd like to know how you'll stop it," said Frazier, defiantly. "You won't be so mean as to 'skin' a room-mate, and get 'cut' by the whole class for doing it, will you?"

Alas for Geordie! Frazier's penitence had been too short-lived, his escape from the toils in the

ENFORCED TRAMP IN THE AREA ON SATURDAY AFTERNOONS

rifle case too easy, his triumph in French and mathematics too much for his selfish and shallow nature. On his own account, Graham had not received a report for three weeks; on Frazier's he had received five, and these necessitated his writing explanations and wasting time, even though the reports were removed. But one evening, coming in just before call to quarters, he found half a dozen of his class-mates sitting with Frazier and sharing his cigarettes and applauding his stories. Even after the bugle blew, they loitered about going. Under the strict construction of the regulations of the academy it was his duty to order the smoking stopped at once, and to report every cadet engaged in it, but only the cadet officer of the day is "on honor" to report every breach of regulations coming under his notice. That night, in the midst of his frantic efforts to fan out the smoke, in came Lieutenant Allen. The next evening the report was read out, "Graham, orderly, tobacco smoke in quarters 7, 7.30 P.M." "I've simply got to take the punishment," said Geordie, "because I did not stop it the instant I got in." And when Connell and others took it upon themselves to tell Frazier he ought to go to the commandant and assume the responsibility, that young gentleman replied, "You must be sick! I was only one of the lot; 'tisn't as though I did it all alone."

But Foster was one of the party, and Duncan another. These two boys marched up to Colonel Hazzard two days later and declared themselves the smokers, and begged that Graham be relieved; but Graham, as ill-luck would have it, had already been sent for and asked what he had to say.

"Nothing, sir," was his answer.

"If it occurred in your absence, Mr. Graham," said the colonel, kindly, "and you did not see the smokers, or if you put a stop to it the moment you did—"

But Geordie shook his head. And so for six consecutive Saturday afternoons, armed and equipped as a sentry, and thinking unutterable things as he did so, Geordie Graham tramped up and down the area of cadet barracks as punishment for having permitted smoking in quarters. It carried him, in punishment, almost up to Christmas; but there was no lack of company. Some afternoons the area was crowded.

CHAPTER XII

October came and went. The Highlands were all aflame with the gorgeous hue of the autumn foliage. The mountain air was crisp and keen, full of exhilaration and life. Regular hours, regulated exercise, sound sleep were all combining to bring about among the plebes the very "pink of condition." Letters from the far frontier, coming regularly, gave Geordie comfort and encouragement. Both his father and Mr. Mc-Crea bade him be of good cheer, and all would come well. He used to steal away to a quiet nook near Kosciusko's Garden to read his mother's loving missives in those days, for there was little peace for him at home. Benny was developing a new trait with an old name—"boning popularity," it used to be called. The episode of the cigarettes had caused among all thinking members of the Fourth Class much unfavorable comment at Frazier's expense, and he was quick to note the coldness and aversion.

"See here, Pops," said he, "if you think I ought to go and tell the commandant I was smoking, I'll do it; but it isn't going to help

you, that I can see. It's all the fault of these
brutal regulations, making you responsible because you were too much of a gentleman to come
in and order that smoking stopped in your room
right off. If my confessing my part in it would
remove your punishment, I'd do it quick as a cat
can jump—but it couldn't, so what's the use ?"

Graham shook his head, and Frazier magnified
that into proportions which enabled him to say
to many a class-mate, " I offered to go and assume the whole responsibility provided I didn't
have to name the others, but Graham begged
me not to do it."

And now, by way of retaining his hold on the
class, Benny became a lavish entertainer. Many
an evening he would invite certain of his cronies to come up after supper and " bring the
crowd," as he expressed it. It meant that another instalment of luxuries had been received.
It was an easy matter for his fond parents to
send box after box of fruit, confectionery, or
goodies of some kind to " Mr. Peter Peterson,"
at Highland Falls, and for " Mr. Peterson" to
fetch them up the back road west of the ob-
servatory, and down the hill behind the barracks, where, under cover of darkness, Benny
and his chums could meet him and run the " con-
traband" up to the room. Cadets were permitted
to receive an occasional box from home, but not

in such frequency, or without inspection by the officer in charge. And so while Pops and Connell and Ames, and other solid men of the class, were taking their evening stroll before study hour, Benny and his set were feasting and smoking in barracks, but smoking no more when Graham was orderly.

"I don't mean to make any trouble about this case," Pops had said, very quietly, "but I give fair warning I will take no more demerit and punishment on other men's account."

Benny confided to his fellows that Graham was a close-fisted, selfish Scotchy, as he ought to have had sense enough to know he would be. He was sorry he had chosen him as a tent and room mate, but he couldn't leave him now, when Graham so needed his help in mathematics, and there were not a few who accepted his statement as both plausible and probable. Up in the first section, however, the keener minds were "getting on to Frazier," as Connell expressed it, and along about the middle of November a thing occurred that set them all to thinking.

By this time the class was hard at work in a more difficult and intricate part of the text, and the ground was not so familiar to the prize scholar of Beanton. Frazier had to study, and he didn't like it. Up to this point his easy flow of language and his confident mien, coupled with the thorough mathematical drilling he had had at home, had stood him in excellent stead. He was leading the class at an easy gait, and winning the highest mark without much effort. "He can't help being head in French, too," said his friends, "but if he land anywhere in the 5's, he's sure of the head of the class." But about this time Ames and Wheeler began to crowd him. They were "maxing through," while Benny showed an occasional 2.9, 2.8, and once "Old Scad" had actually had to cut off three-tenths from his mark. An admirable and patient instructor, he had one or two defects, as have most men. He was a trifle deaf, and decidedly unsuspicious. An honorable gentleman himself, he was unprepared for the faintest deception in others. Twice had the section noted that when up on questions Frazier was taking advantage of this, for when asked in a tone which clearly indicated that the answer as heard or understood was an error, Benny had, in repeating the answer, changed his words accordingly. Connell, naming no names, asked Mr. Otis and Mr. Glenn if this were considered fair. "No, sir; emphatically no, sir," was the reply.

One Friday night, with a lesson for the morrow that was unusually intricate, Frazier sat chuckling over an amusing book he had smuggled into barracks, while Pops was painfully laboring at

"'I'LL TAKE NO MORE DEMERIT ON OTHER MEN'S ACCOUNT'"

his slate. Next morning at breakfast some one asked Benny how he "worked out the rule" in a certain case, and Benny laughingly answered:

"I haven't even looked at it yet."

"Well, then, you'd better be doing it," was the reply.

Frazier had counted on the fact that for three days past he had been up at the front board on the lesson of the day, and that there was no possibility of its happening this Saturday morning. If called up at all it would be on the work of the previous day. At any rate, after breakfast would be time enough. But so difficult was the demonstration, that when he fell in with his section he had not been able to finish it. That day was signalized by many a "cold fess" in the lower sections; but they were forgotten in view of what happened in the first. Connell and Harris in succession had faced about with "clean boards."

"I can do anything else in the lesson, sir, but not that," said the latter.

But "Scad," was not appeased. "This ought not to occur in the first section," he said. "That 'll do." Then looking around, as though searching for some one to do justice to the subject, his eye fell on Benny. "Mr. Frazier, take that demonstration."

And with a cold chill darting up his legs Benny

went to the board. It was barely 8.30; there was no hope of stringing out his work so as to have it unfinished and unmarked when the bugle sounded. That might do in the fifth section, but not in the first. Keeping up his bold, confident manner, he chalked briskly away, but trusting—praying—something might happen to help him through. Ames, at the next board, was deep in his own problem—a long, intricate matter. Nine o'clock boomed from the old tower, and still these two leaders faced their boards and figured away. At last Benny could see that Ames had skilfully and perfectly solved his problem, and that in the natural order of things he would be called on to recite as soon as Benton finished. Then would come his turn, and for the life of him he could not remember an important equation, on which everything depended — he, Frazier, the cadet so confidently booked for the head of the class! Then Benton began to stumble, and "Old Scad" went over to the board to explain. Ames finished his work, laid aside his chalk, dusted his fingers, gave a downward pull to his coat and an upward hitch to his trousers, picked up the pointer, and was about turning, when Frazier's hand touched his sleeve. On the board before him Benny had chalked as much of the needed equation as he remembered, followed by an interrogation mark.

An appealing glance told what was wanted. Ames glanced anxiously about him, hesitated, colored, then impatiently took up the chalk, and while Scad's broad blue back was turned, rapidly wrote the missing links. Frazier copied, nodded gratefully, and went on. The claimant for the head of the class had sought and obtained and availed himself of the assistance of a rival. Scad neither saw nor suspected. The entrance of the professor of mathematics, making the rounds of his class, led to an exhaustive explanation of some difficult points in the day's lesson. Then Ames began reciting on his problem, and before he finished the bugle recall came ringing through the corridors.

"That 'll do, Mr. Ames; that 'll do, Mr. Frazier. Section's dismissed!" said Scad; and Benny was saved.

"It may do in the fifth section, by gum! but never in the first," said Wheeler and others that evening. "If Frazier comes out head, it's fraud, and nothing less."

But Benny held that as he didn't recite it made no difference. Yet when Monday came it was found that he had been marked 3 for the work which, had he been cross-examined, he could have explained only partially, on which but for Ames's aid he would have failed disastrously. Frazier's mark for the week was higher

13

than that of the class-mate at whose expense and personal risk Benny was saved.

"I'd rather be the foot of the class with your reputation, Pops, than head of the corps with Frazier's," said Connell, hotly, for Geordie was low in his mind. He had been given a hard demonstration that very morning, had failed, and now was fearful of going down another section.

And now, except weekly inspection and occasional guard duty, there were no formations under arms. Drills were discontinued. Study hours were longer. So were the lessons. The snow-flurries became frequent. The dark, dreary winter days were upon them. Geordie took his regular exercise, and was beginning to be looked upon as one of the likeliest athletes in the class. The gymnasium of those days was a primitive affair, but the instructor knew his business, and taught it. All the plebes began to look forward with eagerness or apprehension to the midwinter turning-point—the January examination. Once more, finding himself losing ground with his class, Benny was devoting himself to Pops. There is nothing more ephemeral than popularity, and no place were it counts for so little as West Point. Plebe leaders and idols sometimes hold their sway beyond the winter solstice, but rarely last till June. Then, little

INSPECTION

by little, men who were hardly noticed at the start begin to come forging to the front with the backing of solid respect, and these are the "stayers." When December came many a plebe had far more jovial greeting for Benny than for his grave, reticent room-mate. But the "solid men" of the class—fellows like Ames and Connell, Benton and Ladd and Wheeler—sought the latter more and more with each succeeding day.

At last came the January examination. Geordie had been holding his own at moderate average marks for nearly a month, and knew that he was reasonably safe. Still, a bungling performance would be sure to throw him far down in the class, even though it did not throw him entirely out. He had been faithful, steadfast, systematic, and his honest work was beginning to tell. There was mad excitement in the class over the publication of the rolls. The result as to the head of the class was a foregone conclusion. Warned by his narrow escape in November, Frazier had "turned to" and really studied for several weeks, during which time his performance was brilliant, and even those of his class-mates who neither trusted nor respected him were forced to admit that, so long as he chose to work and leave nothing to chance, he could take the lead and keep it. "But wait till next year, and he's beyond his depth in calculus," said upper class men.

One clear, cold evening in January Mr. Glenn's voice was taxed to the utmost. For nearly forty minutes, with the long line of motionless gray overcoats for an audience, he read through sheet after sheet, page after page, of class standing in all manner of subjects. Our interests are only with the plebes. Despite lapses in discipline, Cadet Frazier led the Fourth Class in general standing. Some eighteen young fellows at the opposite end were declared deficient and discharged, and Geordie Graham found himself No. 38 out of 79 examined and passed. It was really better than he had hoped.

Then began the long pull for June. Each day the sun rose earlier and stayed up longer. Geordie plodded on at his books steadily as ever, cheered by the glad letters from home, and taking comfort in the growing friendship of such fellows as Connell and Ames. Benny, elated with easy victory, had relapsed into his careless, defiant ways. Reports were frequent; explanations ditto. Rumors of allegations against reporting officers and assertions of innocence on Frazier's part "more ingenious than ingenuous" were again afloat. By the time March was ushered in his array of demerit, despite his explanations, was such that Geordie felt concerned, and gravely remonstrated. Frazier, ever intolerant of advice from anybody, resented Pops's interference. "It's all the fault of such outrageous rules and spying officers," said he. Already the plebes were eagerly canvassing the prospects for chevrons in June. Rumors of all kinds were afloat. The faintest hint dropped from the lips of such magnates as the cadet captains or adjutant went from mouth to mouth like wildfire, growing as they flew. "Connell, Forbes, Ames, and Pops were sure of chevrons," said the boys. Indeed, Pops was getting rid of that part of his name now, and being jocularly hailed on all sides as "corporal"; but the finest officer of the Beanton Battalion was not so much as mentioned in cadet prophecies. Of course, they might have to make the head of the class something, but he had a good many demerit, and, what was more, was by no means certain of the head of the class again. He made beautiful figures in geometry and trigonometry and beautiful translations in French. He was "way up" in conversation, but he slipped occasionally in conjugation and grammar. The most fluent and easy speaker of the French tongue, Benny's mark was already lower than those of two young gentlemen who had never been abroad at all.

Then came another matter that showed the drift of public sentiment. A time-honored custom was the election of hop managers for the coming summer. There were to be nine from the new First Class and six from theirs, and canvassing was already lively. Benny renewed his hospitalities, and sought to extend the circle of his guests, for of the former lot no less than six had been among the victims discharged. He began showing attention to many a class-mate hitherto unnoticed. He had a confidential, caressing way of twining his arm around the boy he desired to win over as they walked off together, and all his arts were put in play.

The election was scheduled for the 15th of March, and despite the wintry and blustering weather the Hon. Mr. Frazier and his accomplished wife came from Beanton, bringing with them two very pretty cousins of Benny's, really charming girls, and Benny marshalled his classmates up to the hotel to see them on Saturday and Sunday, Pops blushing like a rose when Mrs. Frazier took his hand and said how glad she was to know the soldierly room-mate of whom her dear boy had told her so much. Doubtless the fond mother thought how very fortunate Geordie was in being Benny's friend.

Altogether the little visit was a big success. Despite the open refusal of many to vote for Frazier, it was held that a young man with his social advantages could not fail to reflect credit upon the class. Enough ballots, therefore, were cast to barely squeeze him through, the lowest of the six.

"I'm sorry they didn't name you as one of them, corporal," he said; "but I suppose you fellows from the frontier don't go much on society."

And, as usual, Pops quietly grinned without making any reply, and, election over, Benny soon fell back into his old ways.

We must jump now to June. All through May Benny had been "bracing up for corporalship," for he could not but note how utterly his claims were ignored by his own class-mates, while Pops kept on in the same steadfast line of duty, always prompt and alert, but silent; so reticent, in fact, and so halting at times in recitations, that he was looked upon by his instructors as slow. Delightedly the whole corps doffed the sombre gray and donned the white trousers on the 1st of June. Review and reception of the Board of Visitors went off in the usual finished style. The examinations of the graduating and furlough classes were rushed swiftly yet searchingly to their close, the Fourth Class sections being taken up rapidly, and disposed of in the same cold-blooded, business-like style, and then, one glorious June morning, the whole corps marched as escort to the graduates to the front of the library, where the diplomas were presented with much ceremony and congratulation. Then back to the front of barracks they tramped and re-formed line, and Glenn's voice rang out the last order he was destined to read as adjutant of the corps of cadets. All appointments hitherto existing in the battalion were annulled, and the following announced in their stead : To be captains, cadets so and so (Pops's first sergeant among them). To be adjutant, Cadet Blank. Then a list of lieutenants, another of sergeants, and then, to the thrilling interest of Geordie and his class-mates, now become full-fledged yearlings, the list of corporals. Cadets Benton, Wright, Ames, and Connell, the first four; Harry Winn, eighth, Graham somewhere below the middle ; Benny Frazier nowhere. The January head of the class was unplaced on the soldier list, and three days later was officially announced to have fallen from first to fourth in general standing.

CHAPTER XIII

YEARLING camp at last! The battalion was re-organized in order to equalize the four companies. The graduates and furlough-men—the latter their tormentors of the previous year—were gone, and Pops wrote to his father and McCrea that the hardest thing he had had yet to do was to say farewell to Glenn and Rand and his own captain, Leonard—the three First Class officers whom he and the plebes generally so greatly admired. Otis, too, was another with whom he found it hard to part. He didn't know how good a friend he had in him until after he was gone. Then an odd thing happened.

The furlough-men's turn came next, and hilariously they were rushing about the area, shaking hands right and left with the objects of their annoying attentions of the year before. Benny Frazier was loudly and conspicuously fraternizing with every older cadet, including a number whom he was wont to declare nothing on earth would ever induce him to speak to. Pops and Connell, shyly conscious of the glisten and glory of their new chevrons, were standing a little apart at the steps of the third division, waiting for the dinner-drum to beat, when Connell, for the first time, as senior non-commissioned officer present for duty, was to form the company, Pops assisting as a file-closer. The two fast friends had been designated as acting first and third sergeants respectively. Suddenly Woods, with two of his class-mates, in their "spick-and-span" civilian garb, came bustling by. The others stopped short to congratulate the pair on their chevrons and to add a friendly word or two, and then, to Geordie's surprise, Woods looked him straight in the eye: "Graham, I want to say before I go that I am heartily sorry for my part in our quarrel of last summer, and that you behaved perfectly right. Won't you shake hands?" And in an instant there was cordial hand-clasp, and with a dozen yearlings and furlough-men intermingled about them, there was a general "shake" all round, and patting of one another on the back, and Woods went off happier for the consciousness that at last he had done the manly and chivalrous thing he should have done long before. Otis and Leonard had told him as much, and down in the bottom of his heart he knew they were right. Only it's so hard a thing to do. Not that a gentleman, boy or man, will shrink from begging the forgiveness of one whom he has injured, but because there are always so many, boys and men both, who are

"'WON'T YOU SHAKE HANDS?'"

not gentlemen, to sneer at what they term the "back-down."

And so there were here. Mr. Jennings, cadet private, Company A, of the furlough class, but kept back a few days on account of an accumulation of demerit, and said to be in danger of deficiency in mathematics, was very loud in his condemnation of the proceedings, now that Woods and most of the class were gone, and there was no Glenn to overawe him. The new First Class officers did not like Jennings, but did not know him as thoroughly as did their predecessors. Frazier, however, was the only member of the new yearling class who was at all sarcastic about the reconciliation; but Benny was in bitter mood just now. Few of the departing cadets, graduates or leave men, had troubled themselves to say a cordial word to him. Few of his classmates had expressed regret at his having fallen from the head of the class, and fewer still at his failure to win chevrons. No boy at the Point marched into camp that lovely June morning with such a jealous demon of disappointment gnawing at his heart as did Benny Frazier. It boded ill for himself, for his friends, and for any new cadets who fell into his clutches; for the boy who so loudly and persistently announced the year before that nothing on earth could induce him to say or do a thing to worry a Fourth

Class man was become the very terror of the plebes.

For two weeks, of course, the opportunities were few. The new First and Third classes were sent into camp as the new-comers arrived and were brought before their examiners. The evening the order was given to pack up and store in the trunk-rooms everything not to be taken to camp Pops was busily at work, while Benny, being room orderly, and solely responsible, was smoking cigarette after cigarette, and "chaffing the corporal," as he called it. There came a sudden knock at the door; Benny hurled the stump into a corner, and sprang to the middle of the floor aghast. Such a thing as inspection the last night in barracks had not occurred to him as a possibility, and this time he, not Pops, would have to bear the punishment. He was trembling with excitement and fear, when a drum-boy orderly poked in his head and said Mr. Graham was wanted at the commandant's office at once. Instantly Benny broke forth in angry abuse of the drummer, whom he accused of purposely imitating an officer's knock, and threatened him with all manner of vengeance. The drum-boy, instead of being abashed, looked Mr. Frazier straight in the face, and replied:

"You will kick me down-stairs, will you? You try it if you want to get kicked out of the corps of cadets. I'm not to be abused by the likes of you."

And Pops, amazed at such language from a drummer to a cadet, even though Frazier had provoked it, was still more amazed at the sudden change that shot over his room-mate's quivering face. Geordie took the drum-boy by the shoulder and put him promptly out into the hall.

"You know better than to speak to a cadet in that way," he said, quietly, but sternly. "Go back to the guard-house." But the boy replied he had another message to deliver.

"I don't speak that way to any other gentleman in the corps," said he, "but I can't stand that fellow, neither can any of us, and you couldn't either if you knew what we know."

But here Geordie ordered silence, and telling the boy to go about his business and keep away from Frazier, he hurried down-stairs. At the office were the commandant and Lieutenant Allen, also the new cadet captain of Company B, their first sergeant of the previous year. Presently Winn and Crandal—Graham's classmates—arrived, and the four cadets were called in. It was fifteen minutes thereafter when Geordie returned to his room, his heart beating high with pride and happiness. He had forgotten for the moment the episode of the drummer-boy. He went bounding up to the top flight, four steps to the jump, burst in at the door just as the orderly came backing out, stowing something in his pocket. Frazier, still pale and with a deep line between his gloomy eyes, nervously thrust some money between the leaves of a book. Geordie plainly saw it. "I told you not to return here," said he, sternly, to the boy.

"I called him in, Graham," interposed Frazier. "He—he had to apologize for his words, or—get into trouble."

But the look on the drummer's face was not that of dejection as he vanished, and Graham, without a word, began unpacking. Frazier lighted a cigarette and retired to his alcove. For fifteen minutes not a word was exchanged, then, as Graham opened the door, and loaded up with a bundle of bedding and clothing, Frazier spoke:

" Where are you going with that truck now? You've got to take it over to camp in the morning."

" I'm not going to camp," said Geordie, slowly—" at least, not now. And, Frazier," continued he, laying down his bundle, " I've not yet said one word to anybody but yourself about this. I've told you twice that our ways were so different that we did not get along as we should as tent or room mates, so if you want to take anybody else, do so. It 'll be some time before I come into camp, and then I shall slip into any vacancy that there may be. To be perfectly frank, I cannot afford the demerit it costs me to live with you, and — I don't like cigarette smoke."

"Any more than you do me, I suppose," drawled Frazier, interrupting. "Now that you've got your chevrons, and passed to the Third Class, you've no further use for the fellow that helped you to both."

Graham colored. It was so utterly false and unjust.

"I've no word to say against you, Frazier, and you know it. I am obliged to you for what help you gave me, but I don't think I owe either my chevrons or my gain in standing to you."

"Oh, you've had this thing all cut and dried for weeks," said Benny, sneering. "You're simply moving over into Connell's room as a preliminary to moving into camp with him, leaving me to find a tent-mate at the last moment."

"I am not going to Connell's. I am not going to camp. I told you so," said Geordie, gulping down his wrath, and speaking—as he had seen McCrea, when he was very angry—slowly and deliberately.

"Where, then? Where are you going to? Surely"— and here a sudden light dawned on Benny — "surely *you*'ve not been turned out over plebes. You are? *You?* Well, may I be blessed! Listen to this, fellows," he cried, rushing across the hall, raging within himself with envy, baffled hope and ambition, bitter jealousy and remorse, all intermingled — " listen to this: Corporal Pops turned out over plebes!"

"Well, why not?" answered the yearling addressed; while his room-mate coolly demanded:

"What is there that seems ridiculous to you in that, Frazier?" And he, too, went in to congratulate Graham, while Benny dashed miserably down-stairs in search of some one to sympathize with him, and some one to whom to tell the story of Graham's treachery.

" Upbraided Pops for going back on him about the tent, did he?" said Benton after tattoo that night. " Well, the moment it was known, five days ago, that I was to act as sergeant-major this summer, Frazier came to ask me to choose him for a tent-mate and battalion clerk. He can make out a prettier set of papers than any man in the class, but I'd rather do all the work myself, and any fellow can tell him so that likes to."

And so for two weeks after the battalion went into camp Pops remained on duty at the menagerie, proud and happy in the trust reposed in him. He was the junior of the corporals detailed for this important and onerous duty. Under the supervision of Lieutenant Allen and

ON SPECIAL DUTY OVER PLEBES

the command of Cadet Captain Rice, these young corporals, who but a year ago were undergoing their own initiation, were become the instructors and disciplinarians of the new-comers, as well as their defenders against yearling depredations.

To Pops the duty meant ceaseless vigilance in two ways — against his class - mates on the one hand, against himself on the other. He was a believer in the better results to be obtained from a firm, sustained, and dignified system of instruction, as opposed to the more snappy and emphatic methods that had long been the accepted thing among yearling drill-masters. The latter might be more efficacious where drills were few and the squads careless or slouchy; but when drilling three times a day, and drilling boys eager to learn and trying to do their best, Pops had views of his own. At first their duties were to assist and supervise their class-mates detailed as squad instructors, but time and again Geordie found that a few quiet words from him, accompanied by an illustration of the soldierly execution of the required motion, had far more effect than the scolding of his comrades. Presently the squads were consolidated. Then came the eventful day of their march to camp and distribution to companies. The night before this happened Lieutenant Allen took occasion to compliment the cadet captain on his vigilance and management. "And what's more, sir, you were right about Mr. Graham. Both the colonel and I thought him slow and perhaps lacking in force, but he has done admirably."

"Yes, sir," answered Mr. Rice, "and I believe he will be just as efficient in the battalion."

Once in camp, of course, the yearlings not on duty over plebes took every opportunity to play the customary tricks and enforce the usual "taking down" process. Balked in their earlier efforts, a gang led by Frazier became conspicuous in every scheme to humiliate and annoy. The boy who was most petulant and persistent in his complaints of the brutality of yearling language the year before was loudest and most annoying now, as well as the most relentless taskmaster. He was occupying a "yearling den," the second tent from the color-line, with two equally reckless fellows as mates, while Connell, occupying the first sergeant's tent at the east end of the company street, had saved a place for Geordie, who, though continued on special duty over plebes, now slept in his own company. Frazier had made some scoffing salutation as Pops came wheeling in his barrow-load of bedding, but Graham paid no heed. The relations of the previous year were practically at an end.

For the first three or four nights such was the

vigilance of the officers that little active disturbance of the plebes occurred; but at all hours of the day and evening, when the boys were not in ranks or on duty, hazing in some form or other was going on. The hops had begun. The post was filling up with visitors. Many of the corps had friends and relatives at the hotels or among the families on the post. Benny, a beautiful dancer, and bright, chatty fellow, was basking in the sunshine of his social triumphs outside of camp and revelling in mischief within. By the 8th of July Graham had a squad of thirty plebes to drill and perfect in the manual, and keen was the rivalry between his boys and Crandal's. Geordie had won the respect and was rapidly winning the enthusiastic regard of his recruits. Crandal, far sharper in his manner, was "much more military," as most of the yearlings said, but the officers held different views. Both Winn and Crandal ranked Geordie, as has been stated; yet the Kentuckian, after watching Pops's methods while his own squad was resting, did not hesitate to say, "He holds right over us; we're not in it with him as a drill-master"—a statement which Crandal, however, could not for a moment indorse.

On the 10th of July every man of Geordie's squad was in the battalion, yet forty remained who were declared not yet proficient. Some were

Winn's, some Crandal's, some were the back-sliders from smaller squads, but Winn was relieved, and sent back to the battalion to act as color-bearer, and only Crandal and Pops were left. Four days later Mr. Crandal was returned to his company. "Made too much noise," said Lieutenant Allen, in explaining it afterwards, and Pops was left in sole charge of the backward plebes. Within the week Colonel Hazzard, after critical watching for a day or two, said to Geordie, in the hearing of the sentry on Number Five: "That is excellent work, Mr. Graham. You deserve great credit, sir." And the sentry on Number Five was Benny Frazier, who listened with jealous and angry heart.

Two days later, all plebes being now regularly in the battalion, Geordie was returned to duty with Company B, and the next day marched on guard as junior corporal. He had heard of the arrival of Mr. and Mrs. Frazier with their girl friends the previous evening; and just before parade, among the throng of arriving guests, as Geordie was returning from the post of the sentry on Number Two, he came suddenly upon the party close to the visitors' tent. Throwing his rifle into the other hand, Geordie lifted his shako in courteous salutation. Mr. Frazier senior, walking with Cadet Warren, made a flourishing bow, and in stately dignity said:

" *Good*-evening, Mr. Graham : I hope you are well, sir," but passed quickly on. Mrs. Frazier's bow and the bows of the younger ladies were cold and formal. A lump rose in Geordie's throat. He hated to be misjudged.

"It's all Benny boy's doings," said Connell, angrily, when he learned of the occurrence that night. "That young prodigy is a well-bred, sweet-mannered cad."

It seems, too, that the Honorable Mr. Frazier adopted the same magnificent manner to the senior officers whom he chanced to meet. To them, to whom he could not say too much of Benny's gifts a year gone by, he now spoke only in the most formal and ceremonious way. To certain of the younger graduates, however, he confided his sense of the affront put upon him personally by the omission of the name of his son and heir ("The finest soldier of the lot, sir, as any competent and unprejudiced officer will tell you") from the list of corporals.

But if the disappointed old gentleman would no longer recognize the superintendent and commandant as men worthy his esteem, he was showing odd interest in the humbler grades. Lieutenant Allen, trotting in one evening from a ride through the mountains, came suddenly upon two dim figures just outside the north gate. One, a drummer-boy, darted down the hill towards the engineer barracks; the other, tall and portly, turned his back and walked with much dignity away.

"What's old man Frazier hobnobbing with drum-boys for?" said he to Lieutenant Breeze at the mess that evening, at which query the bright eyes of Lieutenant Breeze blazed with added interest.

"I wish I could find out," said he.

CHAPTER XIV

Augusт came, and the Fraziers went, promising to return for the 28th. Once more all the influences that a mother's love can devise had been brought to bear on those members of Benny's class whose friendship he either claimed or desired. Connell had been besieged with smiles, and would have been overwhelmed with attentions but for his sturdy determination "not to be bought." Then came open rupture. As first sergeant he had rebuked Frazier for falling in with belts disarranged at parade, and attempting to adjust them in ranks. Benny was piling up demerit, and yet taking every possible liberty, and doing a good deal of angry talking behind Connell's back when reported. This time Connell left his place in front of the centre and walked down opposite his class-mate.

"Fall out, Frazier. You know perfectly well you have no business in ranks in that shape. Fall out, and fix your belts." And Frazier, scowling and muttering sulkily, obeyed. Connell overheard something that sounded very like "putting on too many airs; boning military at a class-mate's expense," as he started back to his post, and whirled about, quick as a cat.

"Class-mate or no class-mate, you cannot appear in ranks of this company in that shape, and I want no words about it," he said. Then as Benny, hanging his head and refusing to meet his eyes, bunglingly fastened his belt, Connell went on to the right of the company. They were standing at ease by this time, and as soon as Connell was well out of hearing, Frazier again began:

"You're taking advantage of your size, that's what you're doing, Mr. Connell; and you wouldn't dare to speak to me in that tone if you weren't altogether too big for me to tackle."

Geordie heard this. He could not help hearing it, but before he could warn Benny to say no more of that, the cadet captain called the company to attention, and began his inspection. That night, after tattoo, Connell said to Geordie:

"I hear that Frazier declared I was taking advantage of my size. Did you hear it?" And Pops refused to answer.

"I don't mean to see any more trouble between you and Benny if I can help it, Con," said he. "He's making an ass of himself, but there sha'n't be any row if I can prevent it."

"THE CADET CAPTAIN BEGAN HIS INSPECTION"

But Pops couldn't prevent it. Connell went wrathfully in search of Benny, charged him with what had been said, and demanded that he either affirm or deny it, and Benny could not deny; there were altogether too many witnesses.

"I *am* too heavy to take advantage of you in any way," said Connell, as soon as he could control his temper sufficiently, "but in the whole class or the whole corps I challenge you to find one man who will say I have imposed in the faintest degree upon you. If you can, I'll beg your pardon; if not, by Jupiter, you must beg mine!"

So far from finding any one to agree with him, for even his tent-mates had to admit they thought he deserved all he got, and was lucky in not being reported for muttering when spoken to on duty—a report which carried heavy punishment,—Benny ran foul of a Tartar. Little Brooks, who was slighter and shorter than himself, fired up when Frazier appealed to him, and said: "Connell was perfectly right, and you were utterly wrong. You've been wrong all along ever since we came in camp. You've imposed on him in every way you dared, and simply forced him to 'skin' you, or else stand convicted of showing you partiality. That's my opinion, since you ask it; and if I were in Connell's place you'd eat your words or fight—one of the two."

This was a stunner, as Winn put it. Benny

now had no recourse but to challenge Brooks, as, indeed, Benny himself well knew. It was either that or a case of being "sent to Coventry."

"My parents are here, as you very probably considered when you made your remarks, Mr. Brooks," said he, magnificently. "I do not wish to fight while they're here. They go on Saturday, and then we can settle this."

"Any time you please, only don't wait too long," was Brooks's reply.

But they didn't go Saturday. They stayed several days longer. Meantime Frazier accused Geordie of having reported his language to Connell. He also told his mother of this new act of meanness on Graham's part. Mrs. Frazier could not understand such base ingratitude. If that was the result of being brought up in the army, she hoped her boy would quit the service as soon as possible after graduation. Frazier apologized to Connell with very bad grace. But while that ended hostilities, so far as they were concerned, Connell told him in plain words that he owed still another apology. "You have given your relations to understand," he said, "that it was Graham who reported your language to me. It was Graham who refused to do it." All the same, Benny did not take the trouble to undo the wrong he had done, and set Geordie right with his mother and friends.

The Fraziers were gone by the first week in August, however, and then Benny had a disordered stomach of some kind, and Dr. Brett excused him two days, but sent him about his business on the third, saying there was nothing on earth the matter with him but eating too much pastry and smoking cigarettes. Then Benny had several confinements to serve, and sent word to Mr. Brooks, who was waxing impatient, that there'd be time enough after he got out of confinement and could go to Fort Clinton. Brooks replied that if it would be any accommodation he'd cut supper that evening, and they could "have it out" in the company street when camp was deserted, but Frazier declined. By the second week in August the boy found he was considered a shirk, and in order to prove his willingness to fight he carried his bullying of a shy, silent, lanky plebe to a point the poor fellow couldn't stand. He was taller than Frazier, but had not the advantage of the year's gymnastic training, and Benny won an easy victory, but only over the plebe. It was evident his classmates were still shy of him.

Then he came to Geordie and asked him to be his second, and carry his challenge to Brooks. He wanted the indorsement that such seconding would carry, but Geordie refused.

"Why not?" asked Benny, hotly.

"For two reasons. First, because I agree with Brooks; and second, because you have no right whatever to ask me to second you."

Benny went off, aflame with indignation, to report Graham's monstrous conduct. Some of the class said Geordie was entirely right; others replied that there were plenty to second him even if Pops wouldn't, and at last poor Benny found there was no help for it. He had to meet that fierce little C Company bantam, and he did; but the fight wasn't worth telling about. Benny couldn't be coaxed to get up after the second knock-down. He was scientifically hammered for about thirty seconds, and that was quite enough. He was so meek for a few days thereafter that even the plebes laughed.

And now the foolish boy decided it due to his dignity to "cut Graham cold," which means to refuse to speak to or recognize a fellow-cadet at all—a matter that hardly helped him in his class, and this was the state of affairs between them until the end of camp.

Geordie really felt it more than he showed. He hated to be misjudged, yet was too proud to require any further words. Between him and Connell, Ames, Winn, Benton, Rogers, and men of that stamp in the class the bonds of friendship were constantly strengthening. B Company kept up a good name for discipline during camp, thanks to Connell's thoroughly soldierly work as first sergeant, and the cadet captain's even-tempered methods. Geordie, as third sergeant, had few occasions to assert his authority or come in unpleasant contact with upper-class men serving as privates. He was content, hopeful, happy. He spent one or two evenings looking on at the hops, but the more he looked the more boyish his class-mates appeared as contrasted with the cavaliers he had been accustomed to watch at Fort Reynolds; so he and Connell preferred listening to the music from a distance. On Saturdays they clambered over the glorious heights that surrounded them, made long explorations among the mountains, and had many a splendid swim in the Hudson. They kept up their dancing-lessons "for First Class camp," as they said, and to that they were already looking forward.

At last came the rush of visitors for the closing week in camp, the return of the pallid-faced furlough - men, the surrender of their offices to the *bona fide* sergeants, and Geordie and Connell found themselves shoulder to shoulder in the front rank on the right of Company B. Three days later, and with the September sunshine pouring in their window on the south side of barracks, the two corporals were room-mates at last. Connell being already hailed among his class-mates as "Badger," in honor of his State, the next thing Geordie knew some fellow suggested that there was no use calling him "corporal" when he really was a corporal and would be a sergeant in less than a year, and so, Connell being "Badger," why not find a characteristic name for Pops. "Call him *Kiote*," suggested Fowler, who came from far Nebraska, and gave the frontiersman's pronunciation to the Spanish *coyote* — the prairie wolf. And so it happened that the two Western chums started their housekeeping for the Third Class year under the firm name of "Badger & Coyote."

Meantime Benny Frazier, staggering under a heavy weight of demerit and the ill-concealed distrust of a number of his class, had moved into the room across the hall. Connell and Geordie had hoped they would not find themselves in the same division, but the matter seemed unavoidable. Benny's chum was a college-bred young fellow of some twenty years of age, with a love for slang, cigarettes, and fast society. His name was Cullen. No steadiness could be expected there. Extremes met in the two cadet households at the south end of the third division "cockloft" that beautiful autumn, and, except as extremes, they hardly met at all. There was little intercourse between the rooms. Cullen sometimes came in to borrow matches, soap, postage-stamps, or something or other of that ilk; Benny never.

Studies began at once as they did the previous year, and Geordie started about the middle of the fourth section in mathematics and in the fifth in French. In determining his general standing this year he would have no English study to aid him. He must do his best with analytical and calculus, with French and drawing, and for drawing he had little or no taste. It was with gloomy foreboding, therefore, that the boy began his work, for there was every prospect of his standing lower in January than at the beginning of the term. Frankly he wrote home his fears, and his eyes filled when he read the loving, confident replies. Both father and mother were well content with his record, and bade him borrow no trouble. Even if French and drawing should pull him down a few files, what mattered it?

Buddie was enthusiastically happy, however, for when the revision of the cadet appointments was announced very few changes were made except among the corporals. Benton held his place as first, Connell rose from fourth to third, Ames, more studious than military, dropped a few files, and Geordie made the biggest rise of anybody. From fourteenth he climbed to eighth, jumping among others Crandal, and this in Buddie's eyes was better than standing high in scholarship.

With all his earnest nature Geordie threw himself into the work before him. Connell, with his clear, logical head and steady application, speedily proved of the utmost service to his less brilliant chum, for, so far from resenting request for explanation, he was perpetually inquiring if Geordie saw through this, that, and the other thing, and resenting, if anything, the reluctance of his room-mate to ask for aid instead of wasting time groping in the dark.

"Well," said Pops, "I don't want to give up until certain I can't do it myself, and it takes time."

This in itself was a far better condition of things than existed the previous year. Then there was another. Connell was every bit as orderly and careful as Pops. He held that it was unsoldierly to be indifferent to regulations. From first to last of September neither received a single demerit, and Connell was winning high and Graham good marks in every academic duty.

The autumn weather was gorgeous. The afternoon battalion and skirmish drills were full of spirit and interest. Then came early October, early frosts, gorgeous foliage all over the heights, and, above all, their first lessons in the riding - hall. The year of gymnastic training had measurably prepared them, and Frazier had ridden, so he informed his cronies, ever since he was big enough to straddle a Shetland; he therefore was all impatience to show the class how perfectly he was

THE SKIRMISH DRILLS WERE FULL OF SPIRIT AND INTEREST"

at home *à cheval.* But like many and many another youth, poor Benny found there was a vast difference between sitting a natty English pigskin on a bridlewise and gaited steed, and riding a rough, hard-mouthed cavalry "plug," whose jaws and temper had been wrenched by his abnormal employment as a draught-horse at battery drill. Three days' chafing sent Frazier to hospital, while Pops rode higher into popular favor.

"Coyote may be no mathematician," said Winn, who, as a Kentuckian, was authority on horse matters, "but he can outride any man in this class, by jinks! and give points to many a fellow in the others."

When December came Geordie's patient, steadfast work had begun to tell. Drawing proved no such stumbling-block as he expected. He found himself clumsy at first in topographical work, yet gradually becoming interested and skilful. His score was the exact reverse of Frazier's. Starting with his usual easy dash and confidence, Benny's performances the first few weeks won high marks, while Geordie's "goose-tracks" were rewarded with nothing above 2. As weeks wore on the steadfast workers began to challenge Frazier for place. One after another Benton, Ames, and certain lesser lights climbed above him. Then he grew reckless, and the week before the Christmas holidays Graham's mark

15

was better than that of the quondam head of the class. So, too, in French. Geordie never could succeed in reading or speaking the language in which Frazier was idiomatic fluency itself, but he knew more about its grammatical structure, and his translations were accurate, and even at times scholarly. The January examination, to which Graham had looked forward with such dread, because he believed he must go down, passed off with very different results. He had gained two files in mathematics, ten in languages, and twelve in drawing. As for discipline, he and Connell stood among the very leaders.

"Stick to it, Geordie boy," wrote Lieutenant McCrea, " we're proud of you. I have bet Lane you will be one of the four first sergeants in June and up among the twenties in class rank." As for his mother's letter, Geordie read it with eyes that grew so wet the loving words began to swim and dance, and soon were blotted out entirely.

Then came the long uphill pull to furlough June — that blessed, blissful, half-way resting-place so eagerly looked forward to. If it meant joy to fourscore stalwart young fellows, who for two years had been living a life of absolute routine and discipline, what did it not promise to fond, yearning mother hearts at home—to mother eyes pining for the sight of the brave boy faces so long denied them? To Pops and Connell the days sped swiftly by, because they wasted no hours in idle dreaming. With them the watchword was ever, "Act, act in the living present."

April artillery drills, the dash and whirl and thunder of light battery work, were upon them before they realized it, and away before they· thought it possible. But there was drag and trouble and tribulation in the room across the hall.

Narrowly escaping discharge on account of demerit in January, both Frazier and his roommate began the new year with a whole volume of punishments and confinements. "Extras breed extras" used to be the saying in the corps. There was a time during Christmas holidays when Benny's room was a sort of "open day and night" restaurant, where all the reckless spirits in the battalion were assembled, where demerit seemed to live in the air and be carried like microbes of disease all over the barracks. On May 1st it was known that Frazier had hardly three demerit to run on until the 1st of June, and that calculus had tripped and thrown him as predicted. Down to the second section went the proud head of the year before, and then in the midst of trials at the Point came tidings of tribulation at home. Mr. Frazier senior had been taken strangely and suddenly ill; had suffered from a partial stroke of paralysis. Benny applied for leave for two days. The superintendent telegraphed for particulars, and on reply refused the application. There was no immediate danger, said the physician. There had been business worries and losses, but the stroke was not fatal.

Then Pops and Connell noticed that Mr. Jennings, who still hung on near the foot of his class, was paying frequent visits to Frazier when the latter, being in confinement, could not get out. Twice they heard high words, but in all the excitement of the coming of June and the examinations, the delirious joy of trying on the civilian dress they were now as eager to appear in as they were to get out of it and into " cadets " two years before, Benny's affairs attracted little attention.

At last came graduating day of the First Class, the announcements of the new officers in the battalion, and Pops and Connell, whose chevrons as corporals rubbed one against the other for the last time in the ranks of the color guard that morning, shook hands the instant " rest " was ordered, the centre of a fire of chaff and congratulation.

" The firm of ' Badger & Coyote ' is dissolved," laughed Harry Winn, for Connell was promoted first sergeant of Company D, and Geordie, who called the roll of old K Troop in Arizona when he was but a four-year-old, was destined for a year to do similar service as cadet first sergeant of Company B; "and I'd rather have you than any man I know," said his new captain, Bend, the first sergeant of their company in their plebe camp, that very night.

And then came the result of the examination. Rising to thirty-first in mathematics, thirtieth in French, and twenty-second in drawing, standing among the first in discipline, Geordie was out of the thirties and into the twenties at last; and two days later he and Connell — the happiest boys in all America—were speeding westward together. "First sergeants and furlough-men, Pops," said Con; "who'd 'a' thought it two years ago? Certainly not Frazier."

Alas, poor Benny! Loaded down with demerit, he was held at the Point when his classmates scattered for home.

CHAPTER XV

IF there is a happier time in a young fellow's life than cadet furlough, I do not know where to find it. Geordie's home-coming was something there is little room to tell of in our brief story of his cadet days. Fort Reynolds had improved but slightly in the two years of his absence; even the quartermaster had to admit that, and lay the blame on Congress; but Pops had improved very much—very much indeed, as even his erstwhile rival, young Breifogle, now a valued book-keeper in the First National Bank, could not but admit. Mrs. Graham's pride in her stalwart boy, Buddie's glory in his big brother, and the doctor's stubborn Scotch effort not to show his satisfaction were all matters of kindly comment in the garrison. After a few days, during which he was seldom out of his mother's sight or hearing, she kissed him fondly, and bade him get to his mountaineering again, for she knew the boy longed for his gun and the heart of the Rockies. He could have had half of Lane's troop as escort and companions had the wishes of the men been consulted, but on the three or four expeditions Buddie, at least, was ever with him; and after the long day's ride or tramp the boys would spread their blankets under the whispering trees, and, feet to the fire, Bud's chin in his hands, and adoring Pops with all his eyes, there for an hour or more he would coax his cadet brother for story after story of the Point. In August Connell came out and spent ten delicious days with them — the first time he had ever set foot in any garrison; and it was lovely to see how Mrs. Graham rejoiced in her big boy's faithful friend and chum; how Bud admired, yet could not quite understand how or why, either as scholar or sergeant, Connell could or should stand higher than Pops. He pestered both by the hour with questions about their companies, the other sergeants, corporals, etc. He hung to them by day, and bitterly resented having to be separated from them by night. He could not be made to see why he should not go everywhere they went, do everything they did.

Connell, it must be owned, found Bud a good deal of a nuisance at times, and even brother Geordie's patience was sometimes tried. Bud was too big and aggressive now to command sympathy, otherwise there would have been something actually pathetic in his grievance at not being allowed to accompany the two cadets when they attended certain "grown-up" parties to which they were invited in town. The officers and ladies at the post made much of the young fellows; McCrea could not do enough for them; and as for the troopers, the best horses and the hounds were ever at their service, and old Sergeant Feeny delighted their hearts by always insisting on "standing attention" and touching his cap to the two young gentlemen. This he was not at all required to do, as they were only half-way to their commissions, as Geordie blushingly pointed out to him.

"But it's proud I am to salute ye, sir," said the veteran; "and then don't the regulations say a cadet ranks any sergeant in the army? Sure you and Mr. Connell are my supariors in law if ye are my juniors in years and chiverones."

The officers gave a dance one evening, and Pops and Connell, as was perfectly proper, attired themselves in their newest gray coats, with the gleaming chevrons and lozenge of first sergeants, and immaculate white trousers set off by the sash of crimson silk net. The ladies, young and old, declared the cadet uniform far more effective than the army blue; and some of the young matrons who had first seen their future husbands when wearing the cadet gray were quite sentimentally affected at sight of it again. Then there were three or four very pretty girls at the

"'BUT IT'S PROUD I AM TO SALUTE YE, SIR,' SAID THE VETERAN"

fort, visiting their army home for vacation, and others in town, and all attended the hops; and both Geordie and Connell were thankful they had been so well drilled in dancing. Altogether, they had ten days of bliss they never will forget; and when Connell had to go, everybody at Reynolds saw that Miss Kitty Willet, the major's bonny blue-eyed daughter, was wearing on her bangle bracelet a new bell button that must have come from right over Jim Connell's heart.

And then, all too soon for the loving mother, it was time for Pops to hasten back to the banks of the Hudson, and gird up his loins for the great race of the third year.

" Pops," said McCrea, " you are going back to what I hold to be the hardest of the four years, and going withal to duties which, more than any others in the cadet battalion, call for all the grit there is in a man. A young fellow who does his whole duty as first sergeant *must* make enemies among the careless, the slouchy, and the stubborn in his company. I hold that no position in the battalion is so calculated to develop all that is soldierly and manly in a cadet as that of first sergeant. There are always upper class men who expect to be treated with consideration, even when they set bad examples; then there are yearlings always trying to be '.reekless' just to excite the envy of the plebes. You'll find it the toughest place you ever had to fill; but go at it with the sole idea of being square and soldierly, and in spite of all they may say or do you'll win the enduring respect of the very men who may buck against you and abuse you in every way. As for popularity, throw all idea of it to the winds; it isn't worth having. Teach them to respect you, and their esteem and affection will certainly follow."

Again and again, on the long way back to the Point, Geordie pondered over what his friend had said, and made up his mind to act accordingly.

"Sergeant-major may sound bigger," said Connell, as the two comrades, reunited on the journey, were having their last night's chat together in the sleeper, "but in point of importance in the corps of cadets it simply isn't in it alongside that of first sergeant. My father can't break himself of the old fashions of the war days. He was 'orderly' sergeant, as they called it in '61, and he takes more stock in my being 'orderly' than my being in the 5's."

One day later and they were again in uniform and on duty, and Pops found himself calmly looking over his company, just seventy strong. The very first names he saw gave him a twinge of premonition — Frazier and Jennings. The latter, found deficient in one of his studies and accorded a re-examination in June, had been turned back to join the new Second Class; and he and Frazier had decided to live together in Company B, taking a third-floor area room in the fourth division, while Geordie, with Ames for his mate, moved in opposite Cadet Captain Bend, who occupied the tower room on the second floor. Everybody was surprised at Jennings's transfer from Company A, where he had served three years, to B, with whose captain and first sergeant both he had had difficulty in the past. Moreover, there was no little comment on his living with Frazier, for the few who are known as "turnbacks" in the corps are usually most tenacious about living with some member of their original class. But Randal, the new first captain, was glad to get so turbulent a spirit as Jennings out of his ranks, and Jennings was of such a height as to enable him to fit in very well, as the battalion was sized in those days on the left of A or the right of B.

Frazier's class rank was now only 17. A story was in circulation that he had written to no less than five of the class, begging them to room with him, and promising to "brace up" this year; but this was confidential matter, and the cadets whose names were given could neither affirm nor deny. One thing was certain: Frazier had not been benefited by his furlough. He was looking sallow and out of condition. His father's health showed no improvement, so he told his chums; neither did his father's affairs, but this he told nobody. Like a number of other deluded people, Benny believed wealth essential to high repute.

For the first week no friction was apparent. Pops had speedily memorized his roster, and mapped out his plans for the daily routine. He had to attend guard-mounting every morning now, which took away something like forty minutes from possible study-time, and perhaps twenty minutes to half an hour were needed in making out the morning reports and other papers. On the other hand, he had the benefit of more exercise by day, and a light after taps until eleven o'clock. All through the Fourth Class year cadets are compelled to attend daily gymnastic exercise under a most skilful teacher; after that it is optional, and, as all get a fair amount of out-door work except during the winter months, very many cadets fail to keep up the training of the plebe year. Not so Pops and Connell. Regularly every day these young athletes put in half an hour with the Indian clubs, determined that when the drills were discontinued they would keep up systematic training in the "gym." But within the first fortnight after their return to barracks, Connell, coming over to compare notes as usual, quietly said they might as well add sparring to the list.

"We may need that more than we think, Pops.

That fellow Jennings is stirring up trouble, unless I am mistaken."

Now there are all manner of little points against which a cadet first sergeant has constantly to be warring, or his company will become lax and unsoldierly. Unless promptly and firmly met, there are always a number of old cadets who want to saunter to their places at drum-beat, who will be, if allowed, always just a little slow, whose coats are not buttoned throughout or collars not adjusted when they fall in, who are unsteady in ranks, who answer to their names either boisterously or ludicrously, who slouch through the manual when not actually on parade, holding it to be undignified in an old cadet to observe the motions like a plebe, who are never closed up to the proper distance at the final tap of the drum— in fine, in a dozen little ways, unless the first sergeant is fearless and vigilant, and demands equal vigilance of his assistants, the *morale* of the company is bound to go down. First Class men and yearlings are generally the men at fault; plebes, as a rule, do the best they know how, for otherwise no mercy is shown them.

Very much in this way did the "custom" strike Connell and Pops. What with roll-calls, recitations, riding, and the brisk evening drills and parade, Geordie had no time to think of anything beyond his duties. But Connell said that

Jennings had been over talking to some of his former class-mates, who were old stagers in Company D, and who were doing a good deal of talking now among themselves about the impropriety of appointing as their first sergeant a fellow from the right wing of the battalion who was not imbued with the time-honored tenets and traditions of the left-flank company. First Class men, said they, had always enjoyed certain privileges, as became gentlemen of their high standing, who were to become officers in less than a year, and one day it was decided they should sound Connell as to what his views might be, and the result was not at all to their liking. Connell couldn't be made to see that, because they were speedily to don the army blue, they should meantime be allowed to discredit the cadet gray.

"There's no reason that I can see," said Connell, "why First Class men shouldn't be just as soldierly in ranks as other cadets, and every reason why they should."

Then a B Company committee of two informally dropped in on Pops with a similar query, and got almost the same answer. Whereupon the committee said that the class had taken counsel together on the subject. They courted no trouble whatever, but simply gave Graham to understand that it wasn't "customary" to hold a First Class man in the ranks to the same rigid performance of the manual and the same precise carriage that would be exacted of a plebe. Neither could they be held to strict account in such trivial affairs as falling in for roll-call with coats unbuttoned or collars awry or belts twisted, or for other little matters of the kind, and any reports given them for such would be " regarded as personal." Whereupon they took their leave, and Geordie met Con with a broad Scotch grin on his face.

" Jennings is at the bottom of it all," said Connell. " He wants them, however, to start the move over in D Company, because he can't initiate anything of the kind under Bend. You understand."

" Well, to my thinking, and according to the way I was brought up," said Geordie, " such specimens should be court - martialled and dismissed the service. Men who have no higher idea of duty than that are not fit to be officers in the army."

" We-el," said philosopher Con, " they are boys only a little older than plebes, so far as knowledge of the world is concerned. The more I look at it the more I see just how comically juvenile we are in a way. When we were plebes, dozens of our class were never going to speak to those fellows of the yearlings, and never, never going to devil plebes. Within a year most of us were hobnobbing with the class above and lording it over the class below. As yearlings, lots of our fellows hated the first sergeants, who made us stand round, and we weren't going to have anything to do with them. Now we who are sergeants not only mean to make the yearlings toe the mark, but the First Class men as well, and they are going to force a fight on us for doing the very thing that in three or four years from now any one of their number who happens to be on duty here as an instructor will report a first sergeant for not doing. The whole corps says that when '*it*' comes back here as an officer it won't forget it ever was a cadet, as every officer seems to do the moment he gets here, and you can bet your sash and chevrons it will do just exactly as the officers seem to do to-day. Now these fellows have an overweening idea of their importance because they are so soon to be graduates. That seems something very big from our point of view, and yet about the first thing a second lieutenant has to learn when he gets to his regiment is that he doesn't amount to a hill of beans. He's nothing but a plebe all over again. There's Jim Forester; when he was cadet officer of the day and we were plebes, didn't we think him just a little tin god on wheels? Recollect what a bully voice he had, and how he used to swing old D Company? But what did he amount to at Fort Reynolds last summer? Nothing but a low-down second lieutenant going on as officer of the guard, drilling squads, and—do you remember how the colonel jumped him that morning for some error in the guard list? Why, Geordie, you and I were of much more account at the fort than he was. And now here are these fellows kicking against the pricks. They don't want to be soldierly, because it's too plebelike in view of their coming shoulder-straps. We-el, they've just got to, that's all there is about it. Where are the gloves?"

And with that the two Westerners doffed their coats, donned the " mittens," and hammered away at each other as they were in daily habit of doing, and had been doing more or less for many a month of their Third Class year, Sayers and other experts coaching and occasionally taking hold for a brisk round or two on their own account. It was well understood that both Badger and Coyote were in tip-top trim and training. Meanwhile no trouble occurred in Connell's company worth speaking of, and little of consequence in B, but it was brewing. Three or four seniors had been deservedly reported for minor offences exactly as Geordie said they should be, but they were gentlemen who took it without audible comment and as a matter of course. Then came an experiment. Mr. Curry, a First

16

Class man of rather slender build and reputation, one of the Jennings set, backed deliberately into ranks one morning at reveille, and stood there leisurely buttoning his coat, glancing at Graham out of the corner of his eye. Geordie had just about reached the B's in his roll, and stopped short.

"Curry, fall out and button that coat."

Curry reddened, but did not budge.

Pops budged, but did not redden. If anything he was a trifle paler as he stepped quickly over opposite the left of the company. His voice was low and firm:

"Curry, fall out·at once and button that coat."

Only two buttons were by this time left unfastened. It took but a second to snap them into place. And then—

"My coat is buttoned," said Curry.

"It was unbuttoned throughout when you fell in ranks, and you know it. You also heard my order to fall out, and disobeyed it," was Graham's answer. Then back to his post he went, finished roll-call, reported "All present, sir," to Cadet Captain Bend, who had silently watched the affair, very possibly thinking it just as well to let Graham settle it for himself. And the next night after parade the following reports were read out in the clear tones of the cadet adjutant:

"Curry—Buttoning coat in ranks at reveille.

"Same—Continuing same after being ordered to fall out.

"Same—Replying to first sergeant from ranks at same."

Before Graham had thrown off his belts Mr. Jennings appeared, and with much majesty of mien proceeded to say:

"Mr. Graham, you have taken advantage of Mr. Curry's size, and in his name and in that of the First Class I am here to demand satisfaction."

"Go for Connell," said Geordie, with a quiet nod to Ames.

Next morning Mr. Jennings did not appear at reveille at all. It seems that the demand was honored at sight. Cadet Captain Bend cut supper and risked his chevrons to see that fight. Connell's heart was up in his mouth just about half the time as he seconded his sergeant comrade. It was a long-fought, longer remembered battle, and ended only within five minutes of call to quarters—Jennings at last, as had been predicted two years before, utterly used up, and Geordie, though bruised and battered, still in the ring.

CHAPTER XVI

Time flies at the Point, even in the hardest year of the four, as McCrea had called that of the Second Class. What with mechanics and chemistry, "tactics" and drawing, riding and drills, winter was upon them before our boys fairly realized it. Every day seemed to make Graham feel more assured in his position, and to strengthen the esteem in which he was held. The cabal of the few First Class men had reacted upon the originators like a boomerang. Jennings was in hospital a full week, and Curry walked punishment tours until January. Now, while Jennings was probably not the best man, pugilistically speaking, whom they could put up against the first sergeants, the better men were as sound morally and mentally as they were physically. Some of them expressed regret that Graham felt it his duty to make such serious reports against their class-mate, but it was conceded by every soldier and gentleman that Curry had brought it all on himself. As for Jennings, he richly deserved the thrashing that he had received, and a more humiliated and astonished fellow there was not in the corps. There was no more trouble in Company B. Geordie ruled it with a hand that never shook, yet without the faintest bluster or show of triumph. The First Class men, as a rule, were a very pleasant set, with a pride in their company, a pride in the corps, and a readiness to sustain Graham; and so he and his fellow-sergeants were spared further complication of that description. "In time of peace prepare for war, however," laughed Connell. "There's no surer way of keeping the peace than being ready for anything that may turn up."

Almost before they knew it the short days and the long, long evenings were upon them again. Mechanics and chemistry seemed to grow harder, but Graham had gained confidence and his instructors wisdom. They found that by digging under the surface there was much more to Geordie's knowledge of a subject than was at first apparent, and his mind as well worth cultivating as many a quicker soil. As for the corps, it is remarkable how many there were who knew all along that Jennings was a vastly overrated, overconfident fellow, whose fame was based on victories over lighter weights, and whose condition had been running down as steadily as Coyote's had been building up. In his own class Geordie was now the object of an almost enthusiastic regard, while the plebes looked upon him with hero - worship most extravagant. He had his enemies, as strong and dutiful men must ever have, but they were of such a class as Curry and Frazier and Jennings. "And what decent man in the corps cares for the ill-will of such as they ?" asked Ames. "It's proof of a fellow's superiority."

Midwinter came, and one day Frazier was "wired" for suddenly. "Bad news from home," said Jennings, in explanation, when the battalion was gathering between the first and second drums for dinner. This time the superintendent did not deny a leave, but extended it a few days to enable the boy to remain for his father's funeral. Benny came back looking years older, sallow, and unhealthy. The broad, deep mourning band on his left arm was explanation of his non-appearance at the Thanksgiving hop. Geordie, Ames, and Connell went over to look on and hear the music.

"We'll have to be doing this sort of thing next year, Pops," said Connell, "so we may as well go and pick up pointers." There were not many girl visitors—at least, not enough for the cavaliers of the senior class, so that many of the corps did not dance at all. About ten o'clock Graham decided he had seen enough and would go home to study a while. The wind was blowing hard from the east. There was a mild, pallid

"GEORDIE, AMES, AND CONNELL WENT OVER TO LOOK ON AND HEAR THE MUSIC"

moon vainly striving to peep through a swift-sailing fleet of scud, and throwing a faint, ghostly light over the barracks and guard-house. Out from the shadows of the stone-wall back of the mess building suddenly appeared a figure in the cadet overcoat with the cape thrown over his head. Catching sight of Graham, and recognizing apparently his step and form, the figure slipped back again whence it came, but not so quickly that Pops did not know it was Benny Frazier. Half a minute later, as he sprang up the steps of the fourth division, he came upon two cadets standing just within the doorway—plebes.

"Oh, Mr. Graham," said one, "the officer of the day is inspecting for men in confinement, and Mr. Jennings and Mr. Frazier are both out."

Not an instant was to be lost. Pops could hear the clink of the cadet sword and the slam of doors in the second division. In two minutes the officer would be over in the fourth, and "Benny and Jenny," as the pair were occasionally termed, would be "hived" absent. Arrest and heavy punishment must surely follow. Pops never stopped to follow the chain of thought. Back he sped on the wings of the wind. Five seconds and he reached the corner. Not a sign of the recent prowler, yet Geordie felt sure he had seen Frazier dart back behind that wall barely half a minute before — engaged in some clandestine bargaining with one of his messengers from the Falls, probably — and Jennings with him. Not a sign of the party down the dark, narrow lane behind the wall, not a sign of them up the grassy slope to the west back of the area retaining wall.

"Frazier! Jennings! Quick!" he called, loud enough to attract their attention if they were near at hand.

No answer.

It was off limits if he ventured either way, west or south, from the corner where he stood, and "off chevrons" if caught. Why risk his prospects for First Class year to save men who had ever been his enemies, and never would have lifted a hand to save him? Only the swaying of the branches and the sweep of the wind answered his excited hail. Not an instant to lose! Bounding up the westward path he ran until beyond the guard-house, and there came suddenly upon a shadowy group of four.

"Back to your room, Frazier! Inspection!" he gasped, halting short.

Two cadets rushed at the word. The two other forms slunk away, as though seeking to hide themselves among the trees up the hill-side. One was a civilian, a stranger to him; the other the drummer with whom Frazier had had the altercation more than a year previous. What were they doing now? Graham never stopped to have a word with them. Quickly he retraced his steps, and succeeded in regaining the area unnoticed. The officer of the day was just coming out of the fourth division as Geordie went in.

"Hello, Coyote! Tired of the light fantastic? or didn't you hop to-night?" he jovially asked.

"Had to come back to bone," was the reply.

It was evident from the cheery manner that nothing had been found amiss. The pair had managed to reach their den in safety, then; yet only in the nick of time. Geordie went to his room and to work, yet the thought of that unseemly stolen interview between Frazier and Jennings, the drummer and the stranger, kept intruding itself upon his mind. Presently a stealthy step came down the stair and to his door. Enter Frazier, still pale, still nervous and palpitating.

"Graham, you did me a great service—me and Jennings—to-night. I—I know—we haven't got along as well as we should, and I suppose I am partially to blame; but I don't want you to think I can't appreciate the risk you ran to save us, though either of us, of course, would have done as much for you—any time. You know that, I hope. We had some business out there, and d-did· you see the others — so as to know them ?"

"I knew the drummer well enough," said Graham, his blue eyes full on Benny's nervous face.

"Well, the other one's a cit. who's doing something for us. Say, one good turn deserves another. Don't tell anybody. about where you saw us, or who were with us, will you? I wouldn't like it to get out on Jennings's account. He's got to work like a dog to graduate, as it is."

And before Graham could answer, in came Ames, astonished at sight of Frazier, and to him Benny began a hurried explanation of how Pops had heard of the inspection, and had rushed down to warn him. Then saying "Remember what I asked you" to Graham, he awkwardly let himself out.

"How are the mighty fallen!" soliloquized Ames, as Benny disappeared. "They say he's going 'way down in both Phil. and Chem. in January. He has no French to help·him now. Benton thinks he'll tumble into the low thirties. What did he want of you?"

"Nothing to speak of," answered Pops, with that quiet grin of his. "He-e—said he came to thank me for giving that warning."

"Oh, thanks be blowed! He never came to thank you, Pops. That was only a pretext. He came to ask you to do or not to do something on his account, and I know it."

So did Geordie, by this time, but could not say so.

Four days after this episode leave of absence from 9.30 A.M. until 11 P.M. was granted Cadet Frazier on urgent personal business. A letter from an executor of the Frazier estate was the means of getting the order. It was known in the corps that, being now twenty-one, Benny was master of some little property, though nowhere near what he had expected would be his own. Making all allowances for the sadness and depression naturally following the loss of a loved parent, it was remarked that every day seemed to add to the trouble and dejection in Frazier's sallow face. He took little exercise, except the enforced tramp in the area on Saturday afternoons. He smoked incessantly. He seemed petulant and miserable in Jennings's society, yet Jennings was his inseparable companion. Wherever he went, there was Jennings. "What in the world is the tie that binds those two?" was the question often asked. They were utterly unlike. Their antecedents were widely opposed. Frazier had been reared in luxury and refinement; Jennings in nobody knew just what. He was the representative of one of the "toughest" congressional districts, originally known as the Sanguinary Second, in a crowded metropolis. He was smart in a certain way that spoke of long association with the street Arab and saloon sports. He was useful in plebe days when his class was standing up for what few rights a plebe is conceded to have, but lost caste as rapidly as his comrades gained wisdom. Only among the few weaklings of the Curry stamp had he a vestige of influence left before the long-expected fight with Graham, and after that and his utter and unlooked-for defeat his name seemed held only in derision. Yet he lorded it over Frazier. "You can hear them snapping and snarling at one another at any hour of the day or night," said their near neighbors. "If Frazier hates him so, why on earth doesn't he 'shake' him? They're getting enough demerit between them to swamp half a dozen men." These comments were almost universal.

By this time Frazier's downward course had brought him, both in philosophy and chemistry, into Geordie's sections. Once in a while he would rouse himself and make a brilliant recitation, but as a rule he seemed apathetic, even reckless. Time and again the young fellow's dark-rimmed eyes were fixed upon his old plebe room-mate's face with such a hungry, wistful, woful look that it haunted Geordie for days. Every time the latter surprised him in the act, however, Benny would turn quickly and deject-edly away. But more than once Graham almost made up his mind to go and beg the boy to say what was his trouble, and let him help him out.

At last the opportunity came. It was just be-fore the January éxamination. Going one night to Frazier's room to notify him of a change in the guard detail, he found Benny alone at the table, his head buried in his arms, his attitude one of hopelessness and despair. He sprang up the instant he heard Geordie's voice.

"I—I—thought it was Jennings," he stam-mered, all confusion. "What's wanted?"

"I came to tell you Ewen would go on sick report, and you'd have to march on guard in his place."

This was said at the door. Then, impulsively stepping forward, Graham laid a hand on his shoulder.

"But, Frazier, I hate to see you looking so miserable. If you're in trouble, can't you let us help you out? There are plenty of fellows left to be your friends. It doesn't become me to say anything against your room-mate, but lots of us think you would do well to cut loose from him."

"Cut loose—from him?" wailed Benny, wring-ing his hands, and turning to Geordie with a look in his dark eyes Pops can never forget. "Oh, if I only—" But there he stopped abruptly, and turned quickly away. Jennings came frowning in, his angry eyes full of suspicion as they glowered at Pops.

"To what circumstance do we owe the honor of this visit?" asked he, in attempted imitation of the theatrical heroes of his acquaintance.

Geordie calmly looked him over a moment, but never deigned reply. Then turned to Benny. "Frazier," said he, as he moved quietly to the door, "any time you feel like dropping in on Ames and me, come, and be sure of a welcome." Then, with another cool glance at Jennings, but without speaking one word to him, he left the room.

That night—a bitter cold December night it was—Pops had just finished telling Ames of the strange state of things as he found them on his visit to Frazier; the tattoo drums were hammering through the area and drowning other sounds; the inspector of the upper subdivision had come down into Bend's room to have a chat with his fellow-officer, when the drums stopped with one abrupt and unanimous slam, and as they did so Graham's eyes dilated, and he sprang to his feet.

A gasping, half-articulate cry and the sound of scuffling feet came from the third floor. Geordie could have sworn he heard his name. Out he went, up the iron stairs he flew, and into utter darkness. The hall light was doused as his foot spurned the lowermost step. Whirling at the head of the stairs, he sped to Frazier's door, other cadets rushing at his heels. There was Benny, with livid face, struggling in the grasp of his burly room-mate, whose muscular hands were choking, strangling at poor Frazier's throat. One blow from Graham's fist sent the big bully reeling across the room; while Benny, suddenly released, fell all of a heap on the floor.

"You brute! How dare you grapple a little fellow like that?" was all Pops had time to say before Bend and his lieutenant came bounding in behind him.

"Back, Jennings! *Down* with him!" ordered Bend, as the maddened "tough" sprang to the arm-rack and seized his rifle. Half a dozen hands collared him before he could draw the bayonet. He backed into a corner, his young captain facing him.

"Stand where you are, sir," was the stern order. "What does all this mean? What has he done to you, Frazier?"

Geordie and Ames were raising Benny by this time. He was faint, bleeding at the mouth and ears, speechless, and out of breath.

"Give him some water and lay him down on the bed. Don't crowd around him. He needs air. Get out, all of you!" and Bend turned on the rapidly increasing crowd. "Back to your quarters!" And then the rattle of cadet swords could be heard against the iron stairway—the sergeant of the guard racing to the scene, followed by the officer of the day.

"He insulted and defied me," growled Jennings, glowering about on the circle of hostile faces. "He insulted my people, my kith and kin. I dare him to deny it, or to tell what led to this. Take your hands off of me, you fellows; I'm no criminal. If you're laying for a thief, there's your game yonder," he said, indicating his prostrate room-mate.

"Shut up, Jennings," ordered Bend; "that's cowardly."

"Cowardly, is it? You'll rue those words, my fine fellow. I thrashed you well once, and I've just been praying for another chance, and now I've got it. Cowardly, is it? By Heaven, you'll smart for that!"

And then, calm and dignified, appeared the officer in charge, Lieutenant Allen. A glance at Benny, still livid and gasping, was sufficient. "Go for Dr. Brett," he said to Ames. Then he turned on Jennings, still backed into the corner, and confronted there by his cool young captain. "There seems to be no reasonable doubt that you are your room-mate's assailant, Mr. Jennings. You are placed in close arrest, sir."

Another night, hours later, the wires flashed a message to the widowed mother, bidding her come to the bedside of her only son.

CHAPTER XVII

January examinations passed by without material change in the standing of those in whom we are most interested, except in the case of Benny Frazier—too ill to appear before the Board. For weeks he had been "running down," and the assault at the hands of Jennings proved but the climax that brought on a violent and dangerous siege of fever. For days the devoted mother, aided by skilled nurses, was ever at the side of her stricken boy. Volunteers from his class, too, were always in readiness as night-watchers; but almost from the first the one for whom he called and of whom he moaned in his delirium was Geordie Graham. No one saw the meeting between the heart-sick, almost hopeless woman and her son's earliest friend and room-mate, but that she had been deeply agitated was plain. From their interview she came forth clinging to his arm, leaning on his strength, and from that time she was never content to have him far away. Each day, between retreat parade and evening call to quarters, there were hours he could spend at Frazier's bedside, and they were the only hours in all the twenty-four that the feeble, childlike patient looked forward to with anything but apathy. For days his life hung in the balance; but when at last the crisis came and went and left him pitiably weak in body and spirit, the one thing he seemed to cling to in life was Graham's brown and muscular hand.

"I wonder I am not jealous," said Mrs. Frazier to the doctor's kindly wife; "but I thank God my poor boy has such a friend left to him, after all his trouble—all the misery into which that—that awful person has led and held him."

And the awful person was Jennings, who, shunned like a pariah by the corps, was again awaiting trial by court-martial as soon as Frazier should be able to testify. For days it looked as though Benny never could appear before an earthly court, and that this case, like the other, must go by default. So long as it appeared that the fever would prove fatal, Jennings kept up his air of bravado and confidence. The evidence of Graham and Ames, the first to reach the scene of the assault, would be sufficient to convict him of that offence, but even they could prove nothing beyond a personal row, said he. It was fully understood, however, that back of all this trouble was the old case of Benny's plebe camp, and that the assault on Graham when a sentry, the stealing of Graham's rifle, and the desertion of Musician Doyle were all matters in which Jennings was a prime mover; and though now "outlawed by the statute"—more than two years having passed since the occurrence of these offences, during which time the alleged offender had in no wise sought to secrete himself from military justice, and therefore a case no longer triable by court‑martial—there is no two-year limit to the contempt of the corps of cadets. They could send him to Coventry at any time, and even though he were graduated it might be impossible to obtain a commission.

But when it was noised about the battalion that Benny was on the mend, and that, day after day, he looked forward to nothing as he did to Geordie's visit, it became known that he had made a full and frank confession, and that Jennings was deeply implicated. Interviewed on this subject, Graham refused to say a word; but Mrs. Frazier had been less cautious. It seemed as though she could not do enough to undo her coldness and injustice to Geordie in the past, or to express her affection and regard for him now. In the overflow of her gratitude and joy, when at last her son was declared out of danger, she told the story to sympathetic lady friends, wives of officers stationed at the post, almost as it had been told to her by Benny, and it was not long in leaking through to the corps. The pent-up wrath of the battalion is not a thing to see and forget. The story flew from lip to lip. "Tar-and-feather him!" "Kick him out!" "Turn him loose and let him run the gantlet!" were some of the mad suggestions, but Bend and cooler counsels prevailed. Realizing his peril, Jennings implored the protection of the commandant, and was given a room in the officers' angle. Then the commandant and adjutant went with Dr. Brett to the convalescent's bed-side, and Benny's statement was reduced to writing.

A few days later the police of Jersey City laid hands on a precious pair. One of them bore the name of Peter Peterson, the other was Doyle, ex-drummer, both wanted for blackmail and other offences, and Doyle for desertion. The news of this capture reached the corps late in the afternoon, and was the talk of the whole mess-hall at supper. Next morning at breakfast came sensation still bigger:

Jennings had fled.

Some time during the night he had packed up such things as he could carry and stolen quietly away. A sentry said he saw a young man in civilian dress, with a bag in his hand, going down towards the south dock about 11 o'clock. He boarded a night train at Cranston's Station, and that was all. It proved the easiest settlement of a vexed case. The court-martial turned its attention to Doyle, the deserter, and Doyle pleaded guilty, for his was a case that was still triable because he had absented himself ever since the desertion occurred. Throwing himself upon the mercy of the court, the boy made his statement. He said that one evening in camp, three summers back, Mr. Jennings was sentry on Number Three, and told him he wanted him, Doyle, to do an errand. Cadets often employed him, and paid him money to carry notes, or to buy cigars, or the like. It was arranged that he was to be there, back of Company A, about ten minutes before tattoo, and, going there, he found a rifle leaning against a tree, and this Mr. Jennings bade him carry out to a point near the east edge of the dump hollow, and look there in the weeds, where he would find, half hidden, another one. The drummers were allowed to cross the post of Number Three without question. He had no difficulty in finding and fetching in the rusty rifle, and left the new rifle in its place, as he had been told, supposing that it was only some trick they were playing. Mr. Frazier was there, inside the sentry's post, on his return, and received from him the rusty gun. That night, later, when he heard the adjutant and the cadet captains talking, he saw the matter was serious and got scared, and went out next day and "found," as he expressed it, what he had left there, and carried it to the adjutant. He was closely questioned, got more frightened, and wanted to tell all he knew; but Jennings swore he would be tried and sent to jail as a thief, and warned him the only safety lay in secrecy. Mr. Frazier gave him ten dollars then to buy his silence, and promised him more; but when Jennings was put in arrest and court was ordered to convene, both Jennings and Frazier were badly scared, and told him there was no hope for him at all if it came to trial, as they'd have to testify to his part in the thing, and that meant penitentiary. Then old Mr. Frazier came and had a talk with him down at the Falls: told him he must get away to save himself, gave him fifty dollars, and promised him employment and immunity from arrest if he would go at once. Doyle told Reilly, another of the boys, of his trouble, and Reilly said he'd better go. He got away all right, but the place Mr. Frazier gave him in Pennsylvania among the miners was too hard work; he couldn't stand it, and asked for more money, and until Frazier died he paid him. Then there was no way but to turn to the cadet, through Reilly, saying he was starving, and would have to come and give himself up and tell all about how the old man had bribed him to desert. Then all of a sudden he was nabbed, and that ended it. No! Cadet

Frazier had never suggested desertion. It was all Mr. Jennings and the father.

And Benny's story corroborated much of poor Doyle's. Jennings had halted him down by the water-tank that wretched night in camp, pointed out how Pops was being shown too much favoritism and getting the "big head." Jennings put him up to getting Graham's rifle—a matter that was easily accomplished in the darkness and the deserted street of Company B; but he never meant it for anything more than a joke, though he was jealous of Graham's success, and did think that he was having too much partiality shown him. Then when Jennings told him to take the rusty rifle to the tent in place of the new one, he wanted to back out; but it was too late. Jennings bullied and threatened him with exposure and dismissal for stealing, etc.—threatened even then to call the corporal of the guard and have him taken to the guard-house, caught in the act. He was bewildered and terrified, and ended by doing exactly as he was told. Then came that dreadful day of investigation, followed later by Jennings's arrest; and then Jennings told him of their desperate plight, and bade him wire for his father to come at once. Jennings told him what to say to his father, and wrote a letter, setting forth what would happen if the drum-boy could not be "fixed," and suggesting how to fix him. His father was utterly dismayed at the scrape that Benny was in, and accepted all Jennings's statements. He did not, of course, consult any of the officers, but carried out everything proposed to the letter. For the time being the boys were saved, but within another year Benny learned from the other drum-boy, Reilly, the one with whom he had had the trouble, that Doyle had let the cat out of the bag. Then he had to bribe Reilly. Then Jennings, too, levied on him, and his father later on, while on furlough; and after his father's death poor Benny's life was one succession of torments. Doyle, Reilly, and Jennings, too, "bled" and threatened him time and again, until in his desperation he sought to make a clean breast of it all to Graham. That night Jennings suspected his object, overtook him in the hall, seized and choked and carried him back, and nearly finished him by strangulation before rescue came. Benny was ready to stand trial—suffer any punishment; but by this time the poor fellow's prostration and penitence, his mother's tears and anxiety, and the fact that he had been throughout the entire history of the affair only a cat's-paw, coupled with the reports of the surgeons that he was in no condition to face a trial, all prevailed. It was late in February before he was sufficiently recovered to be moved about, and then sick leave of absence was granted, and he with his devoted mother left for Nassau. He had parted company with the old class for good and all, and was ordered to report in June and join the class below.

March, spring drills, spring rides, and the election of hop managers for First Class camp, all were upon them again before Benny and his strange and unhappy experiences had ceased to be the universal topic of conversation. Geordie had wonderful letters to write that month, and there had been an interchange of missives between two grateful, prayerful women, one letter leading to another, until now Mrs. Graham's weekly budget to her big boy was full of Mrs. Frazier and the sweet, womanly, motherly letters she wrote. April came, and, despite his modest declination of such an honor, Geordie found himself chosen among the foremost of the nine hop managers for the coming camp. More than that, while study had become so habitual to him that he had risen slowly but steadily even in the most difficult portions of applied mathematics, his progress in chemistry and kindred topics had been still more marked. But, better than all, he was now in the midst of a course wherein no one in all the class was more thoroughly at home. From boyhood, drill and drill regulations, as they are called in this day—"tactics," as they were in his—were matters of everyday acquaintance. He knew cavalry drill "from a to izzard," and the infantry tactics through the school of the battalion thoroughly and well. But all the same he left no stone unturned, no paragraph unstudied, before each day's recitation. Here, at least, were subjects in which he could "face the music" week after week and fairly triumph. And to the delight of Connell, Winn, Ames, Ross, and the first section men generally, it was seen that Geordie was "maxing" steadily through, never losing a single tenth in infantry.

"Go it, Coyote, go it!" said Connell. "By jimminy! there isn't a man in the class that would begrudge you the first place if you can get it." It was even queried whether Ames, to whom maxing in anything now came as easy as failure to some boys, had not deliberately "slouched off" a couple of points so as to secure to Graham first mark in infantry; though, just to make sure of his own place in general standing, he stuck to a solid line of 3's in artillery, Pops following close behind. So far as marks were concerned, therefore, Geordie was certain of high rank in the general subject, for he was as thorough in cavalry as in infantry. Battery books alone presented any novelty to him, and it was conceded that the June examination could not change his prospects.

Meantime, too, as the spring wore on, the members of the Graduating Class seemed to feel that it was due to themselves to behave towards Graham with marked cordiality and regard. Anybody failing in this respect might render himself liable to suspicion of being in some way connected with the old Jennings clique; and no greater shame attached to any member of the corps now than that he had at any time been an associate of that fellow, or even guided by his opinion. On the other hand, to be pointed out as the one man in the corps who had "knocked out" that redoubtable middle-weight was honor that overtopped the chevrons of half the senior class. No one doubted that there were other fellows who could have "bested" the representative of the "Sanguinary Second," but he had wisely refrained from giving them opportunity. Feeling sure of Pops, he ventured once too often, and down went the star of his glory.

May, with its sunshine and showers and long languorous days—"the days of spring fever and spring fights," as the cadets used to say—found the relations between Geordie and his company more and more cordial. All through the year, with absolute impartiality and quiet force, he had done his duty to the best of his ability, and Connell, with all his pride in "old D," was the last to claim for it a superiority over the color company. Bend declared he never had to bother his head about it at all. He marched it out to parade or inspection, but his first sergeant looked to the discipline. Among the officers of the tactical department, too, there was no lack of appreciation of the way in which "McCrea's plebe" had won his way up the ladder of promotion, and the relative position of the cadet officers for the coming summer was already a problem over which the corps was indulging in much speculation and the commandant in no little thought. The two finest positions, as has been said, are those of first captain and adjutant. The former commands the battalion in the mess-hall and on its way to and from the same, while the latter has the most conspicuous part to play at parade, guard-mounting, and the like. The first captain is assigned to the right flank, Company A, and his responsibilities are great. He requires dignity and strength of character beyond the other officers. The adjutant should be a model in bearing, carriage, voice, command, but his duties are more picturesque than formidable. As a rule, these high offices — the captaincies, adjutancy, etc.—are given to cadets whose scholarship and class standing are also high ; for in the greater number of cases soldierly ability and character are there to be found. Yet it often happens that the head of the First Class is only a private in the ranks, and the senior captain or the adjutant comes from the other end of the line. When graduation is close at hand, however, the commandant makes out a list of the recommendations for the coming year, and this he submits to the superintendent. His wishes generally carry all possible weight.

It rarely happens that the first captain is selected from outside the first sergeants of the previous year, and in four cases out of five the office goes to the first sergeant of Company A. The sergeant-major in the same degree is looked upon as a sort of legitimate heir to the adjutancy. He has served as senior non-commissioned officer for a year, and yet has had no opportunity of command other than the few seconds required in forming the guard. He may never have given the command "Forward, march!" He may turn out to have little or no voice, and voice is something an adjutant must have. The first sergeants, on the contrary, have constant use for their lungs and larynx and faculties of command; and it used to happen quite frequently that, to one of these, instead of the sergeant-major, the prize of the adjutancy was given.

But there was no room for doubt in Benton's case, said the corps. He was soldier in every word and action; stood one of the five—*sure;* had a rich resonant voice, that was good to hear in the cadet choir and a delight at the entertain-

ment given the fag-end of February — "one
hundred days to June." No doubt, the plume
and chevrons and sword-knot of the adjutancy
would be his; "and no one," said Badger and
Coyote, "would better grace or deserve it." On
the score of the first captaincy they had less to
say, but the battalion said a good deal. No one
quite understood why, when Ames was dropped
from third to sixth corporal, Wright had not
been dropped from second to eighth or even below. He was a fine, tall, dignified fellow, massive of voice and slow of movement, and a very
hard student. He was "dad" of the class, but
no longer stood in the 5's. He was a fine-look-
ing corporal and would have made an admirable
color-bearer, but his impressive dignity was what
lifted him so high at the start; and, acting as
first sergeant of Company A in their yearling
camp under a famous captain, he made no serious
failure, but could not compare with either Graham or Connell or Winn as a drill-master. He
was made first sergeant of Company A, however, at the outset; and as he was methodical
and massive, things looked all right; but it soon
became apparent that all manner of "breaks"
could happen before his eyes and Wright never
see them. More than that, roll-call with him
was a very perfunctory affair. Time and again
he faced about and reported, "All present, sir!"

when one, two, and even, as once happened, six of his company had slept through reveille. Discipline couldn't help running down in Company A; and when recitations in tactics were about half over, it became evident that Wright was nowhere, compared with Graham and Benton, Ames and Connell, and a dozen more of the class.

"If Wright's made first captain, he'll go to sleep some day, and the corps will march right away from him," said his own cadet captain, who was a frequent sufferer from his sergeant's lapses. "Still, he has the prestige of being first in Company A right along, and nobody can say what Colonel Hazzard or the Supe may do."

But it was decided soon enough.

Back from the beautiful grove, one exquisite June morning, marched the jaunty battalion, each graduate bearing in his white-gloved hand the diploma he had just received in the presence of the revered old general-in-chief, who for the last time addressed the eager audience in cadet gray. Once more the line reformed in the shade of the massive elms in front of barracks. Gray-and-white and motionless, it faced the tall plumed figure of the cadet adjutant, unfolding the last order. Eagerly, impetuously a throng of visitors—men and women, girls and boys—came scurrying after and grouping breathlessly among the trees, all eyes on one form, all ears on one voice. Though he win the highest honors in the highest corps in the army of the United States, not for many a year will that young gentleman be again the centre of such absorbed and universal regard. Quickly he rattles through the orders for the dispersal of the Graduating Class. Who cares for that? They all know that beforehand, anyway. They'll be out of cadet uniform and into cit's in ten minutes from the word "Break ranks!" Here's what all ears are striving to hear. Listen:

Headquarters United States Military Academy,
West Point, N. Y., June 11, 18—.

Orders.
No.........

1. All appointments hitherto existing in the battalion of cadets are hereby annulled, and the following substituted in their stead:

To be captains:
Cadets Graham, Connell, Ross, and Winn.

To be adjutant:
Cadet Denton.

To be quartermaster:
Cadet Ames.

And now Pops is conscious that the trees are

swimming and he is getting dizzy. First captain! first captain! *He?* What will not mother say? What will not Bud say? It is almost incredible. But he gathers himself as the adjutant runs down the list. He sees the smile in Bend's kind face as his loved friend and captain faces about, and for the last time says, "Dismiss the company!" Mechanically his hand snaps in to the shoulder in salute, as for the last time he jumps the old rifle up to the carry, then steps to the front and faces to his left, and finds a frog in his throat as he gives the order, for the last time, to the company he has so well handled throughout the year, "Carry arms!" "Arms port!" "Break ranks, March!" and then is swallowed up in the cheering, hand-shaking, uproarious rush of the whole battalion; is lifted on the shoulders of a squad of stalwart fellows, faithful Connell among them, and borne triumphantly down along the road, and a lane is made through the gang of tossing shakoes, and suddenly a lithe little dark-eyed fellow, in natty suit of summery cits, sends a white top-hat spinning up into the overhanging elms, and clasps Geordie's right in both his dainty kid-gloved hands. "Pops, dear old boy, nobody's gladder than I am!"

And indeed Frazier looks it.

CHAPTER XVIII

WHAT a wonderful summer was that of Geordie's First Class camp! To begin with, even the graduates had helped shoulder him through the sally-port after the announcement of the new appointments, and then turned out in their civilian dress, with canes and silk umbrellas and all manner of unaccustomed, unmilitary "truck," and cheered him, as for the first time he swung the battalion into column and marched it away to the mess-hall; and the new yearlings sliced up the white belts he wore that day and divided them among their number "for luck," and many an appeal came for the old first-sergeant chevrons; but Pops shook his head at that. They went off by mail far out across the rolling prairies to Fort Reynolds, where, in his letter to mother, a few modest words told of the high honor conferred upon him, and that he "thought it should go to Con." Buddie never waited to hear the end of that letter. He bolted, hatless, out of the house and down the line of officers' quarters to tell McCrea, shouting the tidings to everybody he saw as he ran. And McCrea came over to the doctor's forthwith, and Captain Lane and his charming wife dropped in before the family were half through tea; and the colonel came in later to congratulate Mrs. Graham, and so did many another wife and mother during the evening, and it was a season of joy and gladness not soon to be forgotten, and who shall say what volume of praise and thanksgiving and gratitude went up with the loving woman's prayer when at last she could kneel and pour out her heart all alone. Indeed, it seemed, especially to Buddie, an event of much greater moment to the friends on the frontier than it did to Geordie. His first concern was for Connell. Wright, of course—big, ponderous fellow, moving slowly, as big bodies always do—could not be expected to come at once to congratulate the comrades who had stepped over his head. He was "let down easily," however, and made first lieutenant of the company instead of captain; but he came over to shake hands with Graham and tell him it was "all right," and found that Connell had never left his chum from the moment the battalion was dismissed. Brushing his way through the crowd, the loyal fellow had almost fought a passage to Geordie's side. He could not bear the idea that Graham's triumph should be clouded by fear of Connell's disappointment.

"Why, Pops, honest Injun, I'd hate to leave

old D, now that I've got to know them all so well; and I tell you candidly if I expect to land in the Engineers next June I want nothing to interfere with my studies meantime, and first captaincy is a powerful tax on a man's time and thought. But even outside of that, old man, I believe you deserve it more and will honor it more than any fellow in the class."

And with such friends at his back, what young soldier would not feel pride and hope and confidence? Then came the close of the examination, the announcement of class standing; and Geordie had clambered out of the twenties and well up into the teens, standing second in drill regulations (as they are called to-day), third in discipline, well up in drawing, though still in middle sections in the philosophical and chemical courses. Ames was easily head, Benton third, Ross fourth, and Connell fifth. And then came the order to move into camp, and our Geordie found himself, with his second lieutenant for mate, occupying the north end tent of the company officers' row —the tent which, three years before, bucket laden, and with shoulders braced and head erect, he had passed and repassed so many times, never dreaming he should become so thoroughly and easily at home within the white walls, into whose depth it was then profanation to gaze.

Meantime, what of our old acquaintance Benny? All through the months of his sojourn in lovely Nassau the boy had written regularly to the friend of his plebe days, and some of those letters were very characteristic—so much so that Geordie sought to read them to certain of his chums by way of preparing them for Benny's return; but he found all but a very few members of the class utterly intolerant of Frazier. He had "behaved like a cad and a coward," said many of their number, taking their cue from Connell. It was all very well to write and prate about its being the turning-point of his life—starting all wrong—needing all this discipline and distress to set him in the right road. When he had returned and shown by his conduct that there was grit and manliness in him, all right; but the corps never did and never will accept a fellow at his own valuation. He must prove his worth. Benny Frazier might come it over tender-hearted women like Mrs. Doctor Brett and Mrs. Hazzard and Mrs. Other Officials and such dear old dames as Pops himself, but he must "hoe his own row in the corps" was the general saying.

And so even Benny's rush to congratulate Geordie and the impulsive sacrifice of that immaculate tile had softened few hearts. Donning the cadet uniform and silently resuming his place in the ranks of Company B, Frazier strove to ask no favors and resent no coldness. He was not tall enough to join the grenadiers of Company A. There was something pathetic in the big dark eyes as he, a First Class man in years, but a no class man in law, stood irresolute in the company street the day they marched into camp. Yearlings and all had their tents chosen. There was no welcome for him. It was just as well that Mrs. Frazier obeyed her boy's injunctions and kept away until late that summer. For a fortnight or so, until the plebes came into camp, Benny lived all alone. Then, assigned to a tent with Murray and Reed, two cadet privates of the class with whom he had never had dealings and by whom he was treated with cold civility, he made no complaint, nor did he seem to seek their better graces. But Pops never failed to hunt him up if a day went by without Benny's coming to the first captain's tent for a chat. He got Ross to give Frazier a seat at his table in Grant Hall, and would have interceded in other ways, but Frazier himself said no. "I have head enough left to see that I have got to work out my own salvation, Geordie, and you can't make them like me."

And so the humbled fellow kept his own counsel, hearing some pretty hard things occasionally, but saying nothing. The former terror of the plebes in nowise meddled with them now. Mourning for his father was sufficient reason for not attending the hops which, despite his managership, Pops himself very frequently failed to visit. It was lonely work going on guard as the sole representative of an absent class, but Frazier made no remonstrance. There were little points in which he could not overcome the slothful tendencies of his earlier days. He was sometimes late or unprepared, but he took his reports without a murmur and walked post like a man.

The summer wore on. Up with the dawn, out in the sun and the breeze from morn till night, hastening from one brisk martial exercise to another, sometimes in saddle commanding a platoon in the roar and dash of battery drill, sometimes a division in the school of the battalion, sometimes at the great guns of the sea-coast battery, waking the echoes of the Highlands with the thunder of their report and the shriek of the shells towards Target Point, sometimes on the firing-line of the skirmishers, Geordie seemed to broaden with every day, and as first captain he was vigilance itself. "Even in Rand's day you never saw better order or discipline in the hall or in the ranks," said Connell, "and the best of it is, the battalion wants to do as he wishes."

"Coyote & Badger's a close corporation" was yet the saying in the corps, and it was fun to the First Class to hail their senior captains by these Far Western titles. One thing that neither of them would stand, however, was, that any under classman should refer to Geordie as "Pops." That pet name was reserved for the family and very intimate friends.

Connell, to be sure, was one of the gallants of the corps all the summer through, and to Geordie's keen delight his Badger chum seemed to be universally popular in society, and though their tents were at opposite flanks, as were their posts in line of battle, they were seldom far apart when off duty. The two, with Benton, formed what Ames sometimes referred to as the Cadet Triumvirate. Benton made a capital adjutant, and the parades attracted crowds of visitors that, as August evenings grew longer, could hardly be accommodated.

Benny stopped one evening in front of the tent to say that his mother would be up on the morrow. "I have been calling at Dr. Brett's this afternoon, and they expect their relief next week. They've been here four years, you know."

It set Geordie to thinking. Medical officers of the army are seldom if ever kept more than four years at any one station, and his father had now been at Fort Reynolds fully five. Nearly all his professional life had been spent in the Far West. Three or four years he had been shifted about so rapidly and continuously that it was in partial recompense he had been retained so long at this big and pleasant post. "It must be about time for him to be shifted again," thought Geordie, "and now it's bound to be somewhere in the Division of the Atlantic." Odd! not for a whole month had the subject been mentioned in any of his home letters. His father rarely wrote more than a brief note; his mother never less than eight pages; and Bud's productions, curious compositions, were ever a delight to his big brother. But none of these had of late made any reference to change of station. How Geordie wished they might come East and visit the Academy now!

One week later, and the 28th of August was at hand. Camp was crowded, for the noisy furlough-men returned at noon, and were bustling about, making absurd pretence at having forgotten how to get into their "trimmings," and calling for some generous Fourth-hearted Class man to come and aid them. Visitors were swarming all over the post. Hosts of pretty girls had come for the closing hop, and the hotels were crowded to suffocation.

"Your mother promised to 'sit out' three dances with me, Benny," said Pops, as he wound himself into his sash, cadet fashion, as the first drum beat for parade. "Tell her I shall come early to claim them." How he envied the boy his mother's presence! Frazier nodded as he sped away to get into his belts, but with a light in his eyes and a laugh in his heart—very little like the Benny of the year gone by.

"Does Graham make as fine a first captain as we thought he would?" asked a returned furlough sergeant of one of the seniors, as they stood watching him quietly chatting with Benton before the beat of the second drum.

"Tip-top! I don't think there ever was a better one. But from the instant he draws sword in command of that battalion he doesn't know anybody."

Again the long line stretched beyond the flank sentry posts, and last parade in camp went off with the usual snap and spirit in face of hundreds of interested lookers-on. For the last time on that familiar sward the plumed cadet officers of Geordie's class marched to the front and saluted the commander, then scattered to their companies, while the visitors hastened to the waiting vehicles on the surrounding roads. No time could be lost this evening. It was that of the final hop. Ten minutes later, rifles, shakoes, and equipments laid aside, the battalion reformed on the color-line, the officers sprang to their posts, the field-music, still in full parade-dress and white trousers, took station at the left of the long gray line. Geordie whipped the light cadet sword from its scabbard, and his voice, deep and powerful, rang out the commands.

"Continue the march. Companies left wheel, *march!*"

Drums and fifes burst instantly into the liveliest quickstep. Eight beautiful fronts, each pivoting on its left, accurate and steady as sections of some perfect machine, came swinging around into column. "Forward, *march!* Guide right!" and then, "Column half right!" as the leading subdivision completed the wheel. And now away they go over the level Plain, heading for the leaf-embowered gap between the chapel and the old Academic, each subdivision led by its lieutenant commanding, Connell, Ross, and Winn marching as field officers on the guiding flank, Geordie commanding all. Group after group of the gayly-dressed visitors opened out to let them through. The sword arms of the young captains brush close to dainty girlish forms those very arms have encircled in the dance, and pretty faces are smiling into the eyes of those swarthy, sunburned young warriors in whom it would be "unmilitary" to show sign of recognition now. The head of the column reaches the cross-road at the foot of the Plain, and, "Column half left!" Geordie's voice rings out across the level and comes echoing back from the gray walls beyond, and the groups of spectators fall farther back—all but one which, escorted by Colonel Hazzard and Dr. Brett, stands at the edge of the road at the pathway just under the beautiful elms. A lady with soft blue eyes is clinging to the colonel's arm and trembling, despite her every effort. Close beside her stands a grizzled, weather-beaten, soldierly-looking man in tweeds, one hand on the shoulder of a ruddy-faced young fellow who is evidently in high excitement. Just back of them Mrs. Frazier, her dark eyes brimming, is resting on the arm of Dr. Brett. Company after company comes up to the wheeling-point and changes direction almost in front of them, and then, his eyes fixed on his leading guide to see that each sergeant in succession gets his trace the instant the wheel is completed, here comes the brawny, blue-eyed first captain. These returning furlough-men are apt to be a trifle careless in marching, and he means to bring them into shape without an instant's delay. He seems to see nothing outside his command, but when within a dozen yards suddenly he catches sight of the uniforms and of his colonel. Instantly, as soldierly etiquette demands, the blue eyes are fixed on the commanding officer; up comes the gleaming blade in the first motion of the salute, and then—then—what wondrous light is that that all on a sudden flames —transfigures the brave, sun-tanned face? What wild amaze, doubt, certainty, delight, all in a single second, flash into his eyes! What pride and joy! what love and longing! For there, so close that he can almost hear the whisper of his name and feel the spray of the joy-tears that brim in her eyes, stands mother; there stands Buddie, fairly quivering with eagerness; and there stands his father, sturdily striving not to look proud. With every mad longing tugging at his heart and tearing him from his duty to her arms, he as suddenly regains his self-control, lowers his sword in salute, as soldier should, and only quits his grasp upon the hilt and leaps to her side at the colonel's smiling order:

"Fall out, sir; Mr. Connell takes command."

"If that wasn't a low-down trick to play on Coyote, I never heard of one," said Harry Winn that night at supper. "Old Scad never evolved a harder test. Think of parading a fellow's mother at the saluting point when he hadn't seen her for a whole year, just to prove that he's such a soldier he couldn't forget himself even then."

There were lots of boys in gray who believed the whole thing was a "put-up job" to settle a bet among the officers, but they couldn't prove it.

Over the details of that meeting we need not linger. Ordered to assume the duties of surgeon at West Point, Dr. Graham was urged by McCrea and others to give Geordie no warning, but keep it all as a delightful surprise. Neither he nor his gentle wife, however, ever dreamed of its being carried to the point it was. That night when

Grant Hall was crowded, and pretty girls in the daintiest of gowns were dancing with cavaliers in gray and white, in blue and gold, or conventional black, when music and merry laughter and glad voices all conspired to banish care, there was one couple in whose faces—one so sweet, so tender, so full of pride in the stalwart son on whose arm she leaned—there shone a radiance that challenged and then was reflected in every eye.

"She makes me think of Ailie in 'Rab and his Friends,'" said Lieutenant Allen, as he and a group of his fellows stood watching them slowly circling the room.

Man after man of Geordie's class came up to be presented by her big boy, whose cup seemed fairly overflowing. While Bud, painfully conscious of the rapidly liquefying state of his first pair of kids, followed his brother with adoration in his eyes, and Mrs. Frazier, still in deep mourning, could not deny herself the delight of peeping in from the arched entrance, where she and Benny stood for half an hour, "just to see how happy Mrs. Graham looked."

Bless the mother heart! How much joy there was for her after the long exile of the frontier and the three years' separation from her first-born. Speedily they were settled in their new home overlooking the bright blue ribbon of the Hudson, winding down between its bold and beautiful shores. From her windows she could see the front of the gray mess-hall, and day after day hear the tramp of the battalion as it came marching down and Geordie's deep voice ringing out the words of command. She used to drop her needle-work and bustle Buddie, all too willing, from his lessons, and trip away to the Cavalry Plain to watch the evolutions at squadron drill and see her boy—no finer horseman among them all—swinging his sabre at the head of the first platoon, or in the wintry days that speedily set in, slashing at the heads in the riding-hall, and with his nimble fellows wrestling, vaulting, leaping high hurdles, and easily accomplishing feats, bare-back or in saddle, that made her often shudder and turn her eyes away. She loved to stroll out under the arching elms to meet him for a few brief minutes between evening drill and parade, and then watch him and Connell putting their splendidly-drilled companies through all manner of evolutions, as they marched them out to the spirited music of the band. She soon learned the ways of the corps, and loved to have a whole squad of the seniors down to tea each Saturday evening, and was sure to secure the presence of such young damsels as lingered about the Point, so as to make it interesting and joyous for his comrades. Perhaps she would have been less venturesome had she been less sure of Pops, but

"AND SEE HER BOY AT THE HEAD OF THE FIRST PLATOON"

the class declared, "Coyote is spooney over his mother and nobody else." She had dreaded the day that was to take him from her arms to the Point. Now it seemed as though all too soon the day was coming that would take him from the Point, and from her, back to the far frontier he loved so well. The winter fairly flew away. The spring-tide came, and she almost wept the day the ice-gorge went whirling down the Hudson and the whole corps cheered it from the banks above. And the thunder of the guns at the April drills, the volleying of the skirmish-lines in May, were sounds that brought distress to her fond heart, for they told of still another week or month passed by, and only a little space reserved in which, every blessed sun, she could have her big boy at her side.

She went with many another to hear the June examinations. She would not confess it for the world, but if there were only a subject in which Geordie could be declared deficient and turned back to go over the whole year, she would have heard the order without a tear. He had done so well, however, that her friends assured her Geordie would be recommended for the artillery, into which he had no desire, however, to go. She had Mrs. Frazier with her now, and at last Benny seemed to be coming into favor again. He had asked no clemency. He had gone on just as Geordie suggested, and, winning his rank in the 5's of the Second Class, he won what was worth far more—a gradual restoration to confidence in the corps of cadets.

And then McCrea came East on his first long leave, and, mind you, he, an old cadet captain, never lost one point of Geordie's work as commander of Company A. One exquisite evening the long line formed for last parade. Many and many a tear-dimmed eye could be seen among the ladies looking on. The strains of " Auld Lang Syne " were too much for Mrs. Graham ; but she hung a little back, and by the time the brave, bright rank of sixty young soldiers came striding to the front to salute the commandant and receive his brief word of congratulation to them as the Graduating Class, she was ready to smile up into Geordie's face as he hastened to seek her first of all, and then, with his comrades, stand uncovered to receive the salute to them as graduates, tendered by the marching companies on their way to barracks. She sat well back among the throng of visitors and dignitaries on the flag-draped platform when, one after another, the class came forward from the throng of gray-coats to receive the long-coveted, hard-earned diploma. She saw Ames, "as head of the school," greeted with ringing applause by the whole battalion as he faced about to rejoin them. She saw gallant Connell, third in rank, and sure, as he hoped, of the Engineers, turn again to his fellows, for the last time, to be followed to his seat by a storm of hand-clapping that told of the faith and honor in which they held him. And then man after man received his diploma, none lacking kind and cordial greeting from the corps, but arousing no such clamor as that evoked by Connell. Numbers twelve and thirteen and fourteen went back, each with his ribboned prize, and then her heart beat hard in the pause that preceded the next name. She knew just where it would come; but how could she dream what would follow? "Graham!" called the secretary, and, plumed hat in hand, her Geordie rose, and with him, as one man, up rose the corps—classmates and comrades, furlough-men, yearlings, and all. She never heard—I doubt if Geordie could hear—the brief soldierly words of the superintendent in all the tumult that followed. Pops bit his lip and strove to control himself, as he turned at the top step to "face the music" and to meet the eye of every member of his year's command and such a whirlwind of cheers as he had never heard before. Springing down, he strove to regain his old place in their midst; but there was Connell, shouting with the rest, and Benny, stamping and clapping and pounding, and somebody grabbed him on one side and somebody else on the other, and away went his plume, and he threw up his hand waving silence, only to be cheered the louder, for up on the platform were bald-headed members of the Board of Visitors, magnates of the staff, and McCrea and his friends, all applauding, too. For once and at last the corps defied their old first captain, and would not down. Buddie fairly cried with excitement, and the tears, unfettered now, rained down the mother's cheeks. The doctor slipped away from the rear of the platform, and he was found pacing up and down behind the library just as they found him on the river-bank long years before, the evening of the last whipping he had ever given Pops. Geordie looked for him in vain when, a little later, the ceremonies over, he placed his diploma in his mother's hand, and bent and kissed her cheek. "Keep it for me while I go to change my dress," he whispered. "You are the last to say good-bye to the gray. Come close to the first division, so that you may be the first to greet me in cits. And, mother, don't you dare — don't you dare call me lieutenant."

And so, leaving her with McCrea, laughing with a world of gladness, he broke away, his heart too full for further words, his eyes brimming at the thought of all the love and pride and blessing in her face, and up the steps he sprang, halting one instant to wave his hand to her; then into the cool depths of the hall he darted, and we have had our last peep at the gray-clad form of Corporal Pops.

THE END

By ELIZABETH B. CUSTER.

FOLLOWING THE GUIDON. Illustrated. Post 8vo, Cloth, Ornamental, $1 50.

The story is a thrillingly interesting one, charmingly told. . . . Mrs. Custer gives sketches photographic in their fidelity to fact, and touches them with the brush of the true artist just enough to give them coloring. It is a charming volume.—*Boston Traveller.*

Mrs. Custer has the faculty of making her reader see and feel with her. . . . The whole country is indebted to Mrs. Custer for so faithfully depicting phases of a kind of army life now almost passed away.—*Boston Advertiser.*

The book is crowded with the amusing and exciting details of a life strange indeed to those who have spent their time sitting tranquilly at home. Her observation is so quick, her descriptive powers so picturesque, that the camp and the skirmish seem to live before the reader.—*Springfield Republican.*

BOOTS AND SADDLES; Or, Life in Dakota with General Custer. With Portrait of General Custer. 12mo, Cloth, Ornamental, $1 50.

A book of adventure is interesting reading, especially when it is all true, as is the case with "Boots and Saddles." . . . Mrs. Custer does not obtrude the fact that sunshine and solace went with her to tent and fort, but it inheres in her narrative none the less, and as a consequence "these simple annals of our daily life," as she calls them, are never dull nor uninteresting.—*Evangelist*, N. Y.

We have no hesitation is saying that no better or more satisfactory life of General Custer could have been written. Indeed, we may as well speak the thought that is in us, and say plainly that we know of no biographical work anywhere which we count better than this. . . . It is enriched in every chapter with illustrative anecdotes and incidents, and here and there a little life story of pathetic interest is told as an episode.—*N. Y. Commercial Advertiser.*

R. D. BLACKMORE'S NOVELS.

PERLYCROSS. A Novel. 12mo, Cloth, Ornamental, $1 75.

Told with delicate and delightful art. Its pictures of rural English scenes and characters will woo and solace the reader. ... It is charming company in charming surroundings. Its pathos, its humor, and its array of natural incidents are all satisfying. One must feel thankful for so finished and exquisite a story. ... Not often do we find a more impressive piece of work.—*N. Y. Sun.*

SPRINGHAVEN. Illustrated. 12mo, Cloth, $1 50 ; 4to, Paper, 25 cents.

LORNA DOONE. Illustrated. 12mo, Cloth, $1 00 ; 8vo, Paper, 40 cents.

KIT AND KITTY. 12mo, Cloth, $1 25 ; Paper, 35 cents

CHRISTOWELL. 4to, Paper, 20 cents.

CRADOCK NOWELL. 8vo, Paper, 60 cents.

EREMA ; or, My Father's Sin. 8vo, Paper, 50 cents.

MARY ANERLEY. 16mo, Cloth, $1 00 ; 4to, Paper, 15 cents.

TOMMY UPMORE. 16mo, Cloth, 50 cents; Paper, 85 cts.; 4to, Paper, 20 cents.

His tales, all of them, are pre-eminently meritorious. They are remarkable for their careful elaboration, the conscientious finish of their workmanship, their affluence of striking dramatic and narrative incident, their close observation and general interpretation of nature, their profusion of picturesque description, and their quiet and sustained humor. —*Christian Intelligencer, N. Y.*